For Roberta:
Hope you'll enjoy this story from the long ago past about some Westfield folks. Of course, the facts were changed to serve the story but the feelings are "true."
Enjoy.

Kathy

Goodbye, Secret Place

Goodbye, Secret Place

KATHY GIBSON ROE

Houghton Mifflin Company   Boston   1982

Library of Congress Cataloging in Publication Data
Roe, Kathy Gibson.
    Goodbye, secret place.
    Summary: Throughout her first year in junior high
school, Whitney's possessiveness threatens her relation-
ship with her best friend.
    [1. Friendship — Fiction] I. Title.
PZ7.R6227Go   [Fic]   81-20108
ISBN 0-395-31864-5   AACR2

Printed in the United States of America
v 10 9 8 7 6 5 4 3 2 1

Contents

Goodbye,
Secret Place

CHAPTER ONE

The Meeting

"Give us a hand, Whitney." Her father was yanking suit-cases out of the trunk, setting them on the driveway.

Whitney tiptoed up the hot asphalt and pulled two suitcases onto the grass.

"Don't drag them, carry them," her father snapped at her.

Whitney knocked one over as she swayed with the other.

"And pay attention to what you're doing!"

She strained to carry two suitcases at once, the way her father did, to the closed front door. Maybe Charlotte had never gotten her letter? But even if she hadn't, Charlotte's parents knew — they had to know if they were going to let Whitney's family use their house for four weeks. Whitney hated house-hunting, couldn't understand why her parents didn't buy their old house back. She dropped the suitcases, panting, and rang the bell. At least they wouldn't be staying at a motel, her mother had pointed out, and maybe Whitney could convince Charlotte to skip her summer vacation and stay behind to keep her company.

After a while Mrs. Harrison opened the inside door. "Well, I'll be," she exclaimed, pushing open the screen door. "We weren't expecting you till evening."

"Where's Charlotte?"

"Why, Whitney Bennett, not even a hello?"

Whitney smiled to make up for her rudeness, but looked behind Mrs. Harrison, into the gloom, for signs of her old friend. "Is she here?" Whitney couldn't help asking again.

"She's right across the street at Robin's. Hi, Marge." Mrs. Harrison waved to the car. "Can I give you a hand?"

"Robin?" Whitney looked up into the smile that had formed on Mrs. Harrison's face. "Who's Robin?"

"You remember Robin. She used to live way down the street from you."

"Oh, *that* Robin." Whitney stole a glance across the street. "She moved?" she mumbled to herself without caring about the answer.

"Run across the street and fetch Charlotte. Tell her I want her home. She hasn't even *begun* to pack."

Whitney's father approached. Uncertain of what to do, Whitney picked up her two suitcases. Mrs. Harrison took them from her. "Go on."

Whitney turned. Her father stood in her path.

"I'm sending her on an errand, Ben. You mind?"

"Not at all." Her father's voice was gruff, which meant he did mind and who did Mrs. Harrison think she was, interfering with the unloading.

Whitney leapt down the stairs, flew across the street (she'd pay later, but what did she care now?), and halted at the border of the strange front lawn. Now, all of a sudden, she was afraid to see Charlotte again. Why was Charlotte with Robin, anyway? Whitney had never wanted to have anything to do with that kid, although come to think of it, she had never bothered to find out how Charlotte felt about Robin. It hadn't mattered much since Robin was an outsider. She lived across the town boundary and went to another school.

And where was everybody else? Hadn't Charlotte told the gang Whitney was returning? On Whitney's family's departure one year ago the whole neighborhood had been there, even the little kids. But where were they now? The street seemed so deserted. They couldn't be away on vacation, not all at the same time. For a moment Whitney looked down the street in vain for her family's old house on Sherwood Parkway; slowly it registered that the hideous green one with yellow trim right in front of her eyes was it. Five eighty-three. She squinted at the numbers in disbelief. It didn't even look like their house anymore. And the Crosses next door had painted their house too.

Whitney dragged her feet up the cement steps, her heart pounding. She felt short of breath. Her knees

3

started to shake. What if Charlotte wasn't there? She certainly didn't want to see Robin now — Robin Wheeler, of all people. The inside door was open; she thought she could hear laughter upstairs. She slipped her recently acquired glasses into her back pocket before she pushed the button.

"Who is it?" someone shouted.

Whitney felt too nervous to answer. She rang the bell again, peering through the screen. First she saw bare feet, then long legs bounding down the stairs. Without her glasses and through the mesh, though, she wasn't sure who it was, even with the face in full view now.

"Yes?" The girl pressed her nose against the screen from the other side, right into Whitney's, so they were eyeball to eyeball through the screen.

"Is Charlotte here?"

"Yeah, but she's busy. Who're you?"

"Whitney. I used to live up the street from you."

Robin kicked open the screen door. It hit Whitney smack in the face. "Guess who just blew in?" she called up the stairs, holding the door ajar.

Whitney hadn't remembered Robin was so pretty. She had straight black hair and bright blue eyes, lit up, it seemed, with amusement. What was so funny? Whitney wanted to ask. Was Robin laughing at *her*?

"Are you moving back for good?" Robin was staring at her now.

"I guess so. Where's Charlotte?"

"Don't you hate it?"

"What?" Whitney peered around Robin, squinted at the empty stairwell.

"Moving."

"I don't mind it," Whitney lied.

"I hate it. I told my dad if he gets transferred one more time I'm not going."

Whitney snorted. One year ago she had told *her* parents they could go to Alabama without her; *she* wasn't budging.

"Don't believe me. See if I care. *Here she comes...*" Robin sang.

Charlotte slunk down the stairs slowly, her white furry slippers balanced for a moment at the edge of each step, her body posing this way and that in a salmon-colored lounging robe, sashed tightly at the waist.

"...*Miss America.*" Robin winked at Whitney. "I haven't been able to get her to move from the bed all afternoon. She's unbearable."

Whitney could hardly believe her eyes. She was tempted to put on her glasses to make sure it was Charlotte, but she was more self-conscious than ever now about the way she looked herself. Nor, she was sure, could she endure any cracks about her glasses from Charlotte, or from anyone else for that matter. "Hi, Charlotte," she finally managed to get out. "You sure do look different."

"Why, thank you, Whitney, how sweet of you." Char-

5

lotte leaned over and planted a dainty kiss on her cheek before Whitney could get away. She wore exactly the same phony smile her mother had worn at the door.

Whitney felt sick to her stomach. "God, you sure have changed," she said again to fill the silence.

"Yes," Charlotte sighed, rolling her eyes at Robin. "Unfortunately, I have left my childhood behind."

Robin sighed, stuck out her hip, rolled her eyes mockingly. "Ah, yes, it is such a bore to be so adult." Robin turned to Whitney. "Charlotte's the sexiest girl in the seventh grade."

Whitney nodded. She didn't know if she was supposed to laugh or not, if it was true or just a joke. "Your mother wants you," she said to Charlotte, to change the subject.

"Tell here I'll be there shortly. I have to finish today's entry in my diary." Charlotte ran her tongue over her tangerine-colored lips. "Don't they wear lipstick in Alabama?"

Whitney shrugged. "Sure they do."

"Don't let her kid you," Robin interrupted. "Her mother only started letting her wear it in public a month ago."

"You shut up." Charlotte patted the carefully made curls on either side of her face against her cheeks. "Let's get out of here, Whitney. She gets on my nerves. She's just — "

"Jealous." Robin finished the sentence for her. "I can hardly wait to grow up so I can be just like Charlotte B. Harrison." Robin laughed.

Whitney glanced uneasily over her shoulder at the front door, where a tentative scratching had turned into an urgent tearing. Robin wheeled. "Is that your dog?" she asked, a note of wonder in her voice.

"Yeah, I'll take her away," Whitney said apologetically.

"Oh, no," Charlotte and Robin said simultaneously. "Don't do that," Robin finished her sentence while Charlotte said, "Since when have you had a dog?"

"Can I let her in?" Robin pleaded.

"Sure," Whitney said, relieved.

Her dog slipped through the crack, ran to Whitney, then began sniffing the hallway carpet. Robin followed her, trying to pet her back. The dog stopped finally when Robin fondled her ears. Robin stooped in front of her. "You lucky stiff." She sighed, stroking the dog's nose. "What's her name?"

"Lady."

"Lady," Robin murmured at the dog who was wagging its tail and licking her chin.

"She's not usually that friendly with strangers," Whitney noted, half-jealous, half-pleased.

"Dogs love me," Robin assured her, her face buried now in Lady's ear.

"Ugh," Charlotte groaned. "Cats are so much more civilized. I hope you're not planning to bring that mutt into our house?"

Whitney frowned. "Yeah, I was, and she's not a mutt; she's perfectly well behaved, and —"

"It's out of the question. Muffin won't stand for it."

"Muffin?"

"My purebred Angora. And if she's not a mutt, what is she?"

"Welsh terrier." Charlotte didn't challenge her. Whitney took a deep breath. "I'll bet you never even heard of it."

"Does she have papers?"

"Yes," she lied.

"Can I walk her sometimes?" Robin was still nuzzling Lady's ears.

"Maybe."

Charlotte started back up the stairs. "Would you like to read an entry in my diary, Whitney?"

"Nah."

"It's quite interesting."

"I've got to help unpack."

Charlotte stopped again at the top of the stairs. "Really, Whitney, I mean it about that dog. She'll have to stay outside."

"But she can't stay outside. She's never — "

"I'm sure my mother will insist," Charlotte shrilled down the stairwell; then the folds of her robe disappeared into the corridor.

"I'd love to keep her here," Robin offered, "except my brother's allergic."

"Is Charlotte really serious?"

"Probably. Ever since she got her period she's been acting like that."

"Her period?"

8

"Yeah, you know. Have you gotten yours yet?"

"No." Whitney wasn't sure if she should lie or not.

"Me neither. My mother says it's because I don't act ladylike enough, but I think it's because I'm retarded." Robin forced a laugh.

Whitney didn't smile, staring open-mouthed at her. Robin tried to ride Lady, who scooted out from under her and made a beeline for Whitney.

"You want to hear me play the piano?"

Whitney shook her head.

"Do you play? We could do a duet."

She shook her head again.

"Too bad. What *can* you do?"

"Lots of things."

"You want to hear one of my stories? They're hysterically funny."

"No. Thanks." Whitney backed through the screen door. Lady nudged past her, in a hurry to get away too.

"Well, let me at least show you a couple of my drawings. That'll only take a second."

Whitney let the door slam.

"Hey, wait. I've got a great idea." Robin followed Whitney out. "I'll borrow the Samsons' German shepherd and we'll take the dogs to the park. What do you say?"

Whitney hesitated, then glanced down at Lady waiting impatiently at her side.

Robin flew down the steps. "I'll go get Teddy."

"No. I can't, not now."

"Ahhh," Robin picked up a crab apple and chucked it

into the street. Lady bounded after it. "You're no fun either."

"I am too."

Robin kicked another apple with her sneaker; it broke in half. "What *do* you like to do?"

Whitney stared across the street at her parents' empty car. "Maybe we could go tomorrow."

"Yeah, right. Tomorrow." Lady dropped the rotten apple at Whitney's feet. "Can she do tricks?"

"Sure."

"Like what?"

"Sit up, lie down, roll over — "

"Let's see," Robin challenged.

"Not now." Whitney picked up the slobbery apple and heaved it.

Robin followed it with her eyes all the way across the street to the curb. She whistled. "Not bad."

Whitney shrugged. "I wasn't even trying." Across the street Lady nosed around frantically in the high curb grass. Robin eyed Whitney skeptically. Whitney met her stare. What did she see? Whitney wondered. What was she thinking?

"You the only one around here these days?" Whitney broke the stare, unable to stand it any longer.

"What do you mean?" Robin put her hands on her slim hips and looked at Whitney defiantly.

"I mean, where is everybody?"

"Like who, for instance?"

"I don't know . . . Jackie DeFoe, Valerie Atwood, Kendyl Kraft — you know, the old gang."

"They're around. They've got better things to do now than hang out on the streets all day."

"Yeah." Whitney nodded knowingly, then looked puzzled. "Like what?"

Robin burst out laughing.

"What's so funny?" Whitney was indignant.

"Your face." Robin stopped laughing.

"What's so funny about my face?"

"I don't know. It just struck me funny, that's all. One second you looked completely one way, the next completely another."

Whitney frowned. She wasn't sure what Robin was talking about but she *was* sure she didn't like being laughed at. "If you want to see something funny," she muttered for lack of anything better to say, "go look in a mirror." The words fell flat; she regretted instantly having said something so stupid, but it was too late. Robin's face became serious, then looked hurt. All the fun went out of her eyes. "Lady! Here, Lady!" Whitney pretended not to notice. Much to her distress, Lady paid no attention at all to her calls. "Lady! Come here this instant!" Across the street Lady looked up, then went back to her sniffing.

"She doesn't even come when she's called?"

"Of course she does. LADY!" Whitney screamed. "Here Lady, here Lady, heeeere Lady!" Lady trotted up the

Harrisons' driveway past the car, then disappeared under a rhododendron bush.

"Some dog." Robin smirked.

"She has a mind of her own." Whitney started down the front walk. She could feel Robin's eyes on her back. Damn that dog. Now of all times Lady had to ignore her, make a fool out of her. When she got her hands on that dog, she'd wring her neck.

"You should teach your dog to come," Robin called after her, "before you teach her a whole lot of useless tricks."

"At least I *have* a dog," Whitney shouted back. That shut Robin up.

Whitney finally caught up with Lady in the Harrisons' back yard. She yanked her by her choker to the door, Lady whimpering and squealing in exaggerated pain. They got as far as the washroom off the kitchen before Mrs. Harrison stopped them.

"I've spoken to your mother about the dog, dear. We're going to leave her in the car till morning. After that we'll be gone and she can have the run of the house."

"All night?" Whitney gasped. "In the car?"

"You could tie her to the clothesline if you like. But please get her out of here before she devours our precious Muffin."

Whitney dragged Lady back outside. If that's the way they were going to play it, she decided, clinging to Lady's neck on the steps, she'd stay in the car too.

But her mother wouldn't let her stay in the car; not

only that, she forced Whitney to lock Lady up for the night. Whitney explained the situation to Lady and begged her to understand that it was only for this one night, that she wasn't being abandoned forever, but it didn't help. She held her ears to shut out the howling, which didn't stop until everyone had gone to bed and the entire house was dark.

"Did you have a boyfriend in Alabama?" Charlotte propped herself up with her pillow. The two girls were sharing Charlotte's room.

Whitney gazed at the ceiling, her eyes adjusting to the dark. "Sort of."

"Well, Whitney, either you had one or you didn't."

"I had two. How many do you have?" Whitney added quickly.

Charlotte sighed. "My problem is I can't make up my mind which one I like best. Jeff is on the football team but Carl is such a fantastic dancer — "

"Dancer?"

"Yes, that's right, dancer." Charlotte scooped Muffin off the foot of the bed and pressed the mound of fur against her chest. "Don't tell me they don't dance in Alabama?"

"They do, but . . ." The cat's tail brushed across her hand. Whitney had an impulse to yank it.

"But what?" Charlotte rolled her head to the side.

Whitney bit her lower lip. They knew how to dance

all right, but none of them had ever danced with a *boy.*
"But nothing." She flopped to her stomach, covered her
head with her pillow.

"Hey." Charlotte yanked the pillow away.

Whitney grabbed it back. "I've got to go to sleep now."

"You know what I think?"

"No." Whitney covered her head again.

"I think you don't even know *how* to dance."

"I really don't care what you think." Whitney pulled
the ends of the pillow down over her ears.

"You don't, do you?" Charlotte snorted. "Just wait
until I get back from vacation."

"I can hardly wait."

"You haven't changed one bit, Whitney Big Shot Bennett, but everything around here has."

Whitney yawned. "I couldn't care less."

"You'll care all right." Charlotte snuggled down under
the sheet with Muffin in her arms.

Whitney started to tell Charlotte about her cousin who
had won first prize in a dance contest; she was even going to add that he had appeared live on a TV dance
program in Philadelphia but she thought better of it.
(Actually he only believed he was good enough to ap-
pear on TV.) She'd show Charlotte when the time came.

Charlotte's toe tickled her leg. "Don't touch me," Whitney hissed, pushing the foot away.

Charlotte rolled to her edge of the bed. "We wouldn't
think of touching Her Royal Highness, would we, Muffin?" Muffin purred loudly.

"Look who's talking." Whitney scowled.

"You'll be sorry, you'll be sorry, you'll be sorry," Charlotte chanted. Muffin continued to purr.

"Shut up, shut up, shut up." Whitney tried to drown her out, but soon got tired of the drone and stopped. How could this be happening to her? Had they really been friends a year ago? Had Charlotte only pretended always to want to be on her team? Come to think of it, the only reason she had ever liked Charlotte was that Charlotte had seemed so interested in *her*. Well, who needed somebody like that anyway, lolling around in bed all day, writing junk in her diary? But what if Charlotte wasn't the only one, what if they were all like that now? Whitney silently lifted the pillow to stare at her bed partner. "You've got lipstick on your teeth," she said, but Charlotte didn't respond, seemed to be asleep. Well, she wanted no part of it, not of dancing, not of boyfriends, not of Charlotte and her lot.

Charlotte heaved to her side. The cat rolled off her chest and sprawled between them, taking up half the bed. Resisting an impulse to suffocate it, Whitney decided instead to sneak outside to the car and Lady. But she would catch hell for that too. Anyway, in the morning they'd be gone, Charlotte and her sickening airs and stuck-up cat and phony mother. In the meantime Whitney's family would find their own house again, a house they would stay in for good this time. Then maybe everything would be all right.

CHAPTER TWO

Dog Tricks

"Shepherds are too the smartest dogs." Robin patted her full stomach, stretched out under the shade of the Swiss tree.

"No they're not, terriers are," Whitney argued, even though Lady had been unusually stubborn all morning long about coming when she was called. Whitney dug a dog biscuit out of a baggie at the bottom of her lunch bag and held it above Lady's head. "Sit up," she ordered sternly. Lady squatted on her haunches and raised her front paws. "Lie down," Whitney commanded next. Without taking her eyes off the green fish-shaped biscuit, Lady lowered her paws and stretched them out in front of her, easing her stomach to the grass. Whitney smiled. "See?"

"Make her play dead," Robin challenged.

16

Whitney frowned. Robin knew she was having trouble teaching Lady to play dead, something Teddy, the Samsons' dog, did on command, even without the bribe of a biscuit. Lady was standing again, drooling over the biscuit. "Play dead," Whitney said, tapping the grass with the treat. Lady sat. Whitney tapped the ground harder. "Dead. Dead dog." Lady stretched her front legs out again, looked hopefully at Whitney. "DEAD DOG." Whitney enunciated the words clearly, pounding the ground with both hands. Lady rolled to her side but then kicked all fours into the air to throw her weight over and sat back up, waiting expectantly for her reward.

Robin laughed.

"No!" Whitney shouted. "No, no, no. Not roll over. Dead dog."

Lady trotted over to Robin. Robin fondled her ears. Teddy growled and leapt to his feet. "All right, Mr. Possessive. Give her the biscuit, Whitney. At least she tried."

Whitney didn't want to give it to her but felt compelled. "Catch it, Lady." Without hope she tossed it in the air. Lady leapt up, her body twisting in midair as she snapped at the biscuit, catching it in flight. Whitney grinned. "Good dog, Lady."

"Let's face it." Robin took a biscuit out of her lunch bag. "You can't teach an old dog new tricks." Teddy sat attentively in front of her. She placed the biscuit on his nose. They all watched as he sat there, not moving a muscle, the treat balanced right between his eyes. "Catch it," Robin finally ordered. He flipped it in the air, and as it descended he caught it in his open jaws.

"Big deal," Whitney muttered. Never in a million years could she get Lady to do that: sit that still, resist such a temptation. She'd have to try to think of some other trick, one she would secretly teach Lady, then spring on Robin. She tossed another biscuit into the air. "At least Lady has a better disposition than Teddy."

"Mutts always do."

"She's not a mutt."

"She is too."

"She's Welsh terrier."

"She's *part* Welsh terrier. You said so yourself."

"Well, we don't know for sure. She *could* be all terrier."

"Anyone who knows the first thing about dogs, Whitney, can see —"

"So what? What difference does it make?"

"No difference. Just don't go around telling tales about it and expecting people to believe you."

Whitney felt cornered. It wasn't telling tales that bothered her so much; it was getting caught at it. She had to be more careful, think things through. "Do you want to hear this story I wrote?" she asked, to change the subject. She had written it in Alabama and had been wanting to read it to Robin ever since Robin told her that *she* wrote stories.

"I'd rather draw." Robin took out her sketch pad.

"You can draw while I read."

"All right," Robin agreed reluctantly, "but hurry."

The story was twelve pages long, both sides, about a girl who gets lost in the woods with her dog. It took forever to read, but when Whitney was all done, after a long silence, Robin asked, "Is that all?"

"What do you mean, is that all?" Whitney gathered the pages up off the ground.

"I mean" — she said carefully — "it's not even finished."

"That's true," Whitney admitted. Writing even that much had gotten her so tired she had had to abandon the project. "But I plan to finish it."

"I wouldn't if I were you."

"Why not?"

"It's boring."

"It is?" Whitney folded the pages back up and stuffed them into her back pocket.

Robin had propped open her sketch pad on her knees to a clean page. "And besides that," she seemed to be studying something across the lake, "it's babyish."

"Babyish?" Whitney said under her breath, waiting for Robin to go on, but Robin was concentrating on her drawing now. Whitney stood in front of Robin, tried to collect her thoughts. "It may be babyish to you" — she paused, sneaking a look a Robin — "but my mother knows someone at *Seventeen* magazine who's interested in publishing it."

"Move, please." Robin seemed not to be listening. "I'm drawing the lake."

"If you're gonna draw, I'm gonna go."

Robin put down her pencil. "I'll stop."

"I've got to go anyway."

"Don't go." Robin threw her pad aside.

"Got to." Whitney's voice was gruff.

"Wait," Robin pleaded. "I take it back. Your story wasn't *that* bad."

Whitney began walking downstream.

"Where're you going?" Robin looked apprehensive.

"I don't know yet." She turned around and ambled back to the Swiss tree, rested the sole of her sneaker against one of two trunks angling out from a single base. Both trunks were too fat to shinny up, and the lowest branch was far beyond her reach. Whitney considered the climb, began to see a series of footholds up the more horizontal trunk which, if she didn't look down, might get her to the first branch. She began inching her way up, her back against one trunk, her sneakers against the other, until she was stretched out as far as she could go.

"I'll bet I can make it to that branch," she called down to Robin, who was lying on her stomach now, her chin propped in her hands.

"I'll bet you can't," Robin replied automatically.

"How much you want to bet?"

"A million dollars." Robin was on her back now, staring up.

"How about a cupcake?"

"If you do it, I'll do it."

Both Whitney's feet were planted firmly and safely

against the trunk across from her. She could still go back down, avoid risking a fall. But Robin had sat up and was watching attentively. Leaning forward slightly, Whitney planted one foot below her bottom. So far, so good. She took a deep breath, fixed her eyes on the lowest branch across from her, and shoved off. But she was too afraid and didn't push hard enough. She hung in midair over the narrowing space between the two trunks, then she keeled backward, scraping her spine against the rough bark as she fell.

"Are you all right?" Robin peered down at her.

Whitney stood slowly, fighting back her tears; her arm was a little bloody and her tailbone throbbed. "I'm fine," she said angrily as she started back up. This time she pushed off too hard — her stomach rammed into the far trunk, nearly throwing her down again, but somehow she managed to embrace the trunk with her arms, and both sneakers miraculously found footholds underneath her. She ascended carefully now, feeling for new and higher footholds, slipping but regaining her footing on better notches, until the top of her head was just below the lowest branch. For a moment she got stuck. She had no idea how to hoist herself onto the branch without swinging out by her arms, but what if she couldn't get her legs up once she was hanging? There she'd hang until her hands lost their grip and she dropped to the ground. So she clung to the trunk, afraid to go forward, afraid to go back, already starting to get dizzy from the thought of how high she had come.

"Go on," Robin urged, her voice excited now, "you're practically there."

Whitney clawed her way a little higher, until her feet were even with the branch. She closed her eyes so she wouldn't see how far below the ground was, then groped around for something to support her. She felt her foot rest squarely on the branch. The other foot was easy. Slowly she lowered herself until she was straddling the bough. Her legs hung down through the leaves; she gripped the bark of the trunk with her left hand and waved with her right, smiling broadly. "Come on up, it's easy."

Robin was already stretched out between the two trunks.

"Push hard, that's all. You can do it."

Robin pushed and fell. Whitney, who had laid her cheek on the branch to see better, was giving Robin more explicit instructions, when out of the corner of her eye she saw Lady take off across the field and disappear into the woods that separated Route 22 from the open park. Whitney shouted at the top of her lungs, first angrily, then desperately when Lady didn't reappear. Robin had Teddy by the scruff of the neck and was looking anxiously toward the highway. In Alabama Lady had chased cars and Whitney's mother had warned her repeatedly not to let her dog loose anywhere near the highway when she went to Echo Lake Park.

"We'd better go get her." Robin leashed Teddy and began loping across the field.

Then Whitney did a crazy thing. Hands clasped tightly around the branch, she swung around, rocking back and forth upside-down like a possum. Then she let go of the branch with her legs and hung helplessly by her arms until her hands lost their grip and she dropped farther than she'd ever dared to jump. The ground came up so hard and fast it knocked the wind out of her.

She was still gasping for breath when she began limping across the field after Robin. She could hear the cars now and she forgot her sore knee. Running at full speed, she passed Robin at the summit of the hill and crashed through the woods, her heart pounding, her feet flying, until she reached the edge of the highway. She called and called, scanning the road, the woods, the ditch as far up and down the highway as she could see. Suddenly she spotted Lady on the other side of the highway, about to step out in front of the eastbound traffic.

"STAY!" she shrieked. "STAY, LADY, STAY!" But the dog was well out into the road now, trotting gaily toward her. Cars honked and swerved. Lady reached the island and stepped out again, this time directly in the path of an oncoming truck. Brakes screeched. Lady disappeared as the truck swerved around her into the right lane. Whitney bolted off the shoulder onto the asphalt, howling, "Lady, Lady, Lady!" into the roar of the truck. Then the truck was gone. Through the trail of smoke she saw her dog again, still standing in the middle lane.

"Come back," Robin pleaded from the shoulder, but Whitney plunged forward, her eyes on her dog. Tires squealed at her heels. She didn't look, didn't dare to look, until she had her arms around Lady's neck and had lifted her off the road, the honking all around her now. Cars were backed up as far along the highway as she could see. She stood rooted to the middle lane.

"Get out of the road!" someone screamed at her. "Hey, idiot!" A man jumped from his car. "You outta your skull?" He wiped his brow with a handkerchief. "I could've killed you. Don't you know any better?"

It was her shame finally that got her legs going. Body trembling, she carried her dog back to the safety of the ditch. Lady too was shaking all over, and when they fell onto the soft dirt together, Lady trapped underneath her chest, the dog cowered and whimpered while Whitney screamed, "Bad dog, bad dog," and pounded her rump with clenched fists. Robin stood over them, with Teddy on his leash sitting quietly at her side. Whitney didn't want to, not in front of Robin, but she couldn't seem to help herself: she stopped pounding on Lady and threw her arms around the dog's neck, sobbing into her fur. Lady tried to squirm free, but that only made her cry harder, and Robin backed off. Then Whitney stopped, all at once, just as suddenly as she had started.

"Are you all right?" Robin whispered. Whitney didn't answer. She got a firm grip on Lady's collar before she stood. Her legs wobbled. She took a step forward and her knee collapsed under her.

"Hey, let me take Lady. I can hold both of them."

Whitney handed Robin the loop at the end of Lady's choker. They started back through the woods along the path. Lady had her little stump of a tail between her legs, and both Lady and Robin kept glancing up at Whitney. Finally Whitney patted Lady on the head; the stump shot up and wagged. Robin looked relieved but still held tightly to both dogs until they were all the way back to the lake. Only then did she let go, and they all collapsed on the bank at the edge of the water.

They were silent for a long time, gazing into the water, watching minnows as they came to the surface then disappeared again into the muddy depths, when out of nowhere Whitney said, "Know what?" She turned to look at Robin, who was chewing her cuticles.

Robin stopped chewing. "What?"

"I never used to like you."

"No?" She frowned. "Why not?"

"Remember that afternoon you invited me into your house and tried to make me play your slave?"

Robin shook her head.

"Well, you did, and when I didn't want to you said I was a bore and had no imagination."

"That's because you were spoiling the game."

"You *do* remember. I wasn't spoiling anything. You were always trying to lord it over everybody."

"Look who's talking." Robin sat up. "That's just the way you were outdoors. You were always running the show, you and that bully Chuckie Thornton."

Whitney flinched. "Everyone else liked it okay."

"Everyone liked my games too." Robin turned to face her. "Did you have a best friend in Alabama?"

Whitney looked up. Robin was staring intently at her. When her face was serious, the pink part of her lips didn't show at all and she looked like a monkey. Whitney smiled. "I had a lot of friends."

"No, I mean one special friend."

"They were all special," Whitney lied. In fact, none of them had been too special.

"You were lucky." Robin sighed.

"I thought Charlotte was your best friend," Whitney suggested, although she prayed it wasn't true.

Robin skipped a stone across the water. "It's more fun with you."

Whitney looked away, started digging up grass with a stick.

"Hey, I've got an idea." Robin rested her elbow on the ground. "I'll Indian wrestle you."

They lay down on their stomachs. Robin beat her once, twice, three times. Then they leg wrestled and with her good leg, Whitney beat Robin. Angry that she was losing, Robin threw her other leg into the act. Their bodies got tangled and they rolled toward the water, each trying to pin the other, each in her turn coming dangerously close to the edge but escaping in the nick of time. Whitney finally pinned Robin so her head hung over the clay bank. She was laughing at the dogs, who were licking Robin's face, when with an unexpected jerk

Robin freed her arm to tickle Whitney in the ribs. Whitney screamed, half in pain, half in pleasure. Then they were rolling again, away from the shoreline, rolling and tickling and laughing, the dogs barking and snapping at free-flying limbs until the tears ran down the girls' cheeks and their stomachs hurt.

For the rest of the afternoon they lay side by side on their backs, each with a dog stretched out under an arm, pointing out the animal shapes they saw in the great puffy cumulus clouds rolling by overhead. Sometimes the clouds would change before they sank below the trees, sometimes they would stay the same; but neither friend, no matter how hard she tried, could ever quite see what the other one saw so clearly.

CHAPTER THREE

The Pact

"Such waves." The beautician looked longingly at Whitney's hair. "You're a lucky girl."

Whitney nodded mutely. She didn't feel at all lucky.

"How come you want to go and ruin it with a permanent?"

"It's too bushy," Whitney confessed.

The beautician laughed. "Honey, I'd give my right arm for a little bit of that 'bush.' Put your head back." She yanked it down over the sink before Whitney could lower it.

"It's because school's starting next week," Whitney added, as if that somehow explained everything.

"Listen, honey, you want a permanent, I'll give you a permanent. It's your hair." The beautician washed Whitney's hair with a vengeance, and even during the cutting, which had never hurt before, she pulled Whitney's head so hard every which way that the roots started to throb. The set made a still newer pain, little pinches all over Whitney's head from the tight pin curls that were saturated with some cold gooey liquid that leaked down her neck and had a sickening smell, like burning hair.

Once her head was under the giant metal hood, though, the smell went away, and at first the warm buzz felt good. She started reading her latest book, a story about a poor Spanish family that moved to the suburbs and built a house out of scrap tin on an empty lot. When the house was built and they had a vegetable garden planted, they were served with an order to get off the land because they were squatters.

The heat inside her metal helmet had built to such intensity that the pins felt like tiny hot irons burning into Whitney's scalp. A tear rolled down her cheek. Just as the family was about to be run off the lot, someone bought the deed; they could stay if they tore down their tin house and built a proper one that fit in with the rest of the neighborhood. Whitney threw the book down in disgust. Now the tears were really streaming. She slouched in her seat, freeing her head from the scalding prison.

The beautician spotted her attempted escape. "Just a few more minutes and you'll be done." She shoved the contraption down farther so that now even Whitney's eyebrows were covered. Whitney shut her eyes and gritted her teeth. Sweat trickled down the nape of her neck, or maybe it was the goo. Anyway, it was giving her the shivers. She tried to think cold. Right outside the parlor through the Bamberger's Coffee Shoppe was a rest room, where she could submerge her steaming head in a sinkful of icy water.

Just as she was about to make her getaway, her mother reappeared through the glass doors. The beautician rushed over to lift the hood.

"Still drying?" Her mother laid her packages on the magazine table next to Whitney's chair.

"Her hair's thick, ma'am, it took longer than usual. Come with me, dear." The beautician glanced over her shoulder. "This won't take long," she said, smiling at Whitney's mother.

Whitney felt nothing for the next few minutes. Her scalp was so numb she thought her brain must be cooked. When her glasses were finally handed to her, it didn't dawn on her at first that she was facing a mirror. She lifted her hand to her cheek to make sure; still it didn't exactly register. Only when she stood to leave did she begin to experience the full horror of what had been done to her. Tight little springy curls at the ends of frizzy strands of hair, each separated from the other ... her face square now, and all cheek. Blinking back her tears, she turned her head slowly to face her mother. How could you? she asked with her eyes, but her mother was looking away, frowning at the beautician.

"One or two washes and it'll soften. Natural curl doesn't always take well to permanents."

"It looks better than it did before," her mother said

dogmatically on the way home. "At least it's neat." At the dinner table when her father asked her mother how much she'd paid for that rat's nest, she said, "All the girls are getting permanents. It's very feminine, dear," and then, as an afterthought, "It'll grow out in a month or so."

In fact, "all the girls" weren't getting permanents the way they had been in Alabama; they were all wearing their hair straight, and the longer the hair, the better. Her mother said it wasn't her fault the North was behind the South; Whitney just happened to be ahead of the others.

On the first day of school the first words out of Robin's mouth when she saw Whitney's new hairdo were, "Now what did you go and do that to yourself for?"

"It's the latest style," Whitney growled, all the joy of having landed in the same homeroom with Robin evaporating. Whitney's family had moved to another section of town, the Gardens, and although Robin had assured her it wasn't that far and they could bike the mile or so to one another's houses, her parents had kept her so busy unpacking that she had barely had time to see Robin. She began to dread meeting the other kids now as they went en masse to English, math, geography, then split up for gym.

Miss Daniels, a young teacher with a high nasal voice and bright red lipstick, issued gymsuits, instructed them on washing their uniforms at the end of each week for inspection the next week, then dismissed them to the locker room to get their locker assignments and change their clothes. Whitney found her cubicle at the back of an aisle almost immediately, but once her books and bag were safely inside she waited uncertainly while the others milled around looking for theirs.

"I found mine," Robin shouted from several aisles away. Other girls began to fill Whitney's aisle. Roberta Stuart and Beth Hamilton had lockers at the end of the row; they had begun to talk about how pretty Miss Daniels was. Whitney smiled at them but they didn't seem to notice, so she came up behind Roberta, who had been in her Girl Scout troop, and gave her a slap on the back the way her father did when he greeted friends.

"Hey." Roberta whirled. "That hurts."

Whitney's smile faded. "Sorry." She cleared her throat. "It's me. Remember me?"

Roberta blinked.

"Whitney. Whitney Bennett."

Roberta let out a high little scream. "What're *you* doing here?"

"We moved back."

"How come?"

"We didn't like the South."

"But what *happened* to you?"

"What do you mean?"

"You look so *different*."

Beth giggled.

Whitney frowned. "What's so funny?"

Beth looked at Roberta; Roberta gave her a knowing look back. "Whose homeroom are you in?"

"Miss Swan's."

"Oh, you poor thing. We have Mr. Palmer. What a doll and he's so handsome!" Beth giggled again. A bell rang. Someone shouted, "Three more minutes, girls."

Whitney pulled the gym shorts up under the new skirt her mother had made her for the first day of school, then faced the wall, pulling her blouse up over her head. Her undershirt started to come up too, but she yanked it back down. She got stuck again when she tried to shake her arms free — she'd forgotten to unbutton the cuffs. Now Beth and Roberta were both laughing. Whitney wheeled around to frown at them. They were stripped to cotton bras and pants, and Roberta had her hand on her hip. She stopped laughing. "Want me to unbutton your sleeves?" she offered.

Whitney nodded, extending her straight-jacketed arms.

"You sure do have a lot of hair under your arms."

Whitney blushed. Beth giggled.

"Won't your mother let you shave?" Roberta undid the other cuff.

Whitney forced the gymsuit top on over her head. Then she kicked her skirt up off the floor and threw it into her locker.

"Hey, Whitney." Roberta's voice was louder now. "Do all the girls wear undershirts down south?" Other girls in the aisle started giggling. "Allison is the only girl I know of who wears one," Beth chimed in, "but she's as flat as a board."

"What about that girl with a hearing aid?" another voice sang out.

"Beatrice?" Roberta snorted. "She doesn't count."

Robin stood with one foot against the outer wall of their aisle as she bent over her unlaced sneaker. "Hurry up, you guys."

"Last call, girls! Everyone out on the floor."

Whitney pushed through the others to the end of the aisle. "Robin wears an undershirt," she announced.

"She does not."

"She does too. Come on." She grabbed Robin's elbow. "Let's go."

"Wait for us." Roberta ran after them, grabbed Robin's other arm. "Do you or don't you?"

Robin shook her head.

Whitney let go of her. "Prove it."

Robin unbuttoned and spread open the top of her gymsuit. Underneath was a beige stretch nylon bra. Robin touched the tiny pink rose sewn to the band where the cups came together.

Whitney's face clouded. "You never wore one before."

"I did too." She rebuttoned her gymsuit.

"When?"

"All the time."

34

Whitney scowled as she stomped out of the locker room. She'd seen Robin's undershirt, all right. Robin caught up with her under the basketball hoop. "Don't be mad at me. It's different at school."

"I'm not mad." Whitney kicked at the floor.

"It's really not important; why do you take it so seriously?"

"It is important. Why are you wearing that thing now?"

"What's wrong with it?"

"It's . . . it's . . . I don't know, I just thought you . . . Why did you have to lie in front of everyone?"

"Look, I can wear whatever I feel like wearing."

"Line up, girls. On the double. The captain of the cheerleading squad is waiting to talk to you about next week's tryouts."

Whitney ground her toe into the floor. "Are we still going to be friends?" She pouted.

"Is there some reason why we shouldn't be?"

Whitney shrugged, turned her back to Robin.

"Boy, are you acting strange. You want it in writing or what?"

"In blood," Whitney grumbled, trying to hide her hurt, hating herself for being this way.

"All right," Robin said slowly. "We'll make a pact, just like they do in the books."

"When?" Whitney asked skeptically.

"Hey, you two stragglers, this isn't a social hour. Find your places."

"Right after school," Robin whispered, her eyes brightening as they joined the line. "In blood, just like you said."

"Herein, we the undersigned . . . Lady!" Robin stopped writing in her notebook, pushed Lady's nose out of her lap. "What's the matter with her?"

"I don't think she likes the new house."

"Why not?"

"She's not allowed on the furniture."

Lady stood at the base of the stairwell now, whining.

Robin picked up where she left off. *". . . swear to be blood sisters from this moment forward, till death do us part. Signed in blood.* How's that?" Robin handed the notebook to Whitney. Whitney added, *"Violation of this pact will be punishable by death."* Robin recited the entire thing out loud, then whistled under her breath. "I like it. It's even better than the ones in books." She recopied it on a clean sheet of paper, they signed their names, then with a safety pin they pricked one another's index fingers, leaving tiny blood spots next to their signatures. Whitney ran upstairs, Lady bounding after her, to look for a container. When she returned to the basement Robin was sprawled on the couch.

"We'll put the pact in here." Whitney held up a plastic ice-cream container. "Along with a treasure. Something we don't want to give up in the worst way. What do you say?" Whitney and Lady glanced hopefully at Robin.

Robin thought for a moment. "Well, all right, but I'll pick your thing and you pick mine. Otherwise we might not make a real sacrifice."

"Deal. You go first."

Robin leapt up. "Be right back." She dashed upstairs.

Whitney was shocked when Robin came back with the story she'd written. "Why that?" she finally managed to ask, worried that Robin would question the lie she had made up about it. Her mother didn't even know anyone who worked for *Seventeen* magazine, nor had anyone other than Robin heard the story.

Robin shrugged. "You just have to bury it, that's all, and leave it there forever unless we decide to dig it up."

"I thought you said it was no good."

"So what?" Robin stuffed the folded pages into the container. "Now you."

"This isn't exactly fair. What if I want something from your room?"

"We'll bike over, come on."

"No, wait. I've got a better idea."

"What?"

"That thing you're wearing."

"What thing?"

"You know, with the flower on it."

"My bra?"

"Yeah, you bury that."

"You gotta be kidding. What for?"

"Because I want you to. That's the agreement."

"What do I care, I've got more at home." Robin pulled her arms out of her blouse sleeves, wadded the blouse up around her neck, unhooked her bra.

Suddenly Whitney was aware of a car pulling into the driveway. She jumped to her feet. "Quick! Get dressed." The motor coughed and died at the back door. Lady barked, ran upstairs. Whitney stuffed Robin's bra into the container and snapped on the lid.

"Slide it under the couch," Robin whispered.

Whitney was pretending to tie her shoe when her mother leaned over the banister. "How was school? You girls hungry?"

"Starved, Mrs. Bennett." Robin smiled sweetly at Whitney's mother.

"Well, you'll have to come out of that dungeon. And why is Lady whining, Whitney? Didn't you take her out?"

"We were just about to."

Outside on the tree stump they ate mushy apples and discussed hiding places. Whitney was anxious to get rid of the container before her mother discovered it.

"We could bury it in the yard," Robin suggested.

"She'll see us."

"The basement, then."

"She'll find it."

Robin spit an apple seed into the grass. "You want to practice cheers?"

"We have to get rid of this thing."

"After that?"

"I don't know any cheers."

"I'll teach you."

"I'm too tired." Whitney forced a yawn. "But maybe tomorrow," she added, hoping by then Robin would forget. The last thing she wanted to do was spend her free time learning cheers.

"Lady," Whitney's mother bellowed from the door, "come here this instant!"

Whitney scanned the yard. Lady was digging in the rose bed.

"Get her out of there," Mrs. Bennett scolded. "And keep an eye on her. She's your responsibility."

Whitney dragged Lady out of the bushes and back into the house. While she was using the basement toilet she noticed a loose floorboard that ran from the door to the toilet base. She pulled on it. It gave a little. She called Robin and together they tugged until a nail popped out and the board wrenched free. There was a hole nearly a foot deep between the floorboards and the ground. Robin placed the container out of sight under the other boards, Whitney lowered the board back to its place, and then they crawled around on the floor of the tiny cubicle looking for the nail. It was bent. They couldn't force it back down into its hole, and they would make too much noise hammering in a new nail. They decided that Whitney would fix it when it was safe. In the meantime they hoped no one would notice.

As Robin was mounting her bike to leave, she suggested that, to seal the pact "beyond a shadow of a doubt," they exchange rings.

"Why not?" Whitney tried to sound nonchalant, but her heart was racing. She had never heard of exchanging rings; no one had ever proposed such a thing to her before. She watched Robin until she disappeared around the corner, then began wheeling her own bicycle into the garage when she started feeling uneasy all over again. She couldn't quite believe this was going to be for real . . . forever . . . even for long.

CHAPTER FOUR

The Tryouts

On Saturday afternoon Robin's mother pulled into the Bennetts' driveway and honked. It was drizzling. Whitney got out of the house and into the car by the time her mother came out waving her boots and rain hat from the porch. Whitney rolled down the window. "We're late."

"You'll get soaked."

"I'm dry. Besides, Robin isn't wearing boots."

Robin's mother smiled.

"See you later." Whitney rolled the window back up.

Mrs. Wheeler dropped them off in front of their school and Whitney followed Robin into the gym.

"Did you practice?" Robin threw her coat over a metal folding chair.

"No." Whitney threw her coat on top of Robin's. "Did you?"

"No, but I'm beginning to think we should have." She wandered across the gym toward a group of girls, huddled in a circle, talking and giggling.

Whitney did a couple of deep knee bends to stretch her pants. She had worn her tightest jeans and her stomach was beginning to hurt.

"All right, girls," Miss Daniels bellowed from the teachers' entrance to the gym. "Be seated."

Whitney looked around for Robin.

"There you are." Robin broke away from one of the groups and attached herself to Whitney's arm. "Sit with me."

Roberta and another girl Whitney had never seen before sat down at the same time in the empty seat on the other side of Robin. They began bickering over who was there first.

"Let Robin choose."

"No, I was here first." With a thrust of her rump, Roberta pushed the other girl off the edge. The other girl stuck out her tongue at Roberta, then plopped down on the seat next to Whitney.

"Hi, I'm Jane. You a friend of Robin's?"

"Sort of."

Miss Daniels stood in front of them now, frowning. The long row of girls began to quiet down. "Has everyone finished talking?" No one spoke. "That's better. We'll start at this end. Remember to speak loudly and *enunciate* your words. There are only three openings on the squad."

Whitney glanced nervously at Robin, who was staring straight ahead and seemed to be smiling at the empty space between the girls and Miss Daniels. Whitney studied her hand, trying to memorize the words she had written in ink across her palm while she waited her turn. Robin was on the floor now, executing the same cheer she had taught Whitney. When she was done, a few girls clapped. Robin collapsed in her seat. Whitney hid her hand. "I thought you said you didn't practice."

"I didn't," Robin insisted. "It just came naturally."

"Girls!" Miss Daniels shouted. "Try to control yourselves." There was a hush. "Next." Miss Daniels pointed at Whitney.

Whitney rose to her feet.

"Your name, please."

Whitney mumbled her name before peeking one last time at her hand. Miraculously the words came to her, seemed to form automatically with her movements, until, halfway through the cheer, as she was dropping back to the floor from an angel's leap into a one-handed cartwheel she had secretly practiced alone for days, she suddenly forgot the name of her new school. Horrified, she slithered down to the floor into a split. Someone hissed, "Roosevelt," but by then it was too late.

Whitney hunched gloomily in her seat while the rest of the girls had their turns. Several boys had wandered into the gym; they stood behind the chairs in their muddy uniforms with their football helmets tucked under their arms, watching the tryouts. Everyone had been eliminated now except Robin and five other girls. One by one they performed again.

Miss Daniels stood, cleared her throat. "Before I read off the names of the new squad members, I want to thank you all for coming this afternoon. Our incoming class of seventh graders is an especially spirited and talented group and I look forward to having some of you cheering our teams on to victory *next* year." Miss Daniels congratulated the three winners, all eighth graders.

Robin shrugged. "Who wants to hang around with a bunch of snotty eighth-grade girls anyway?" she whispered to Whitney. "We'll start our own cheering squad —"

"Say, you were pretty good."

Whitney turned. A boy from their homeroom smiled benevolently down at Robin.

"Thanks." Robin beamed. "Did you make the team?"

He shrugged. "The B squad. But the coach says I've got potential. I'm just a little out of practice, that's all. Why don't you come out and watch us play?"

"I'd love to." Robin sprang from her chair. Halfway across the gym she stopped, yelled, "C'mon, Whitney," then hurried after him.

Outside Whitney searched the parking lot for her mother, who was always early when she didn't want her but was not there now when she should be, the one time Whitney wanted her to be there. Whitney wandered toward the playground, then saw the boy pushing Robin in a swing. She turned and was on her way back to the parking lot, feeling tricked somehow by her friend, when Robin called out, "Hey, Whitney, watch this."

Whitney stopped and watched Robin. When the swing hit its forward peak, she leaped from her seat, flew through the air, and thumped with a groan onto the concrete. Robin stood up slowly. "Not bad, huh?" She grabbed Whitney's hand, pulling her back to the swing, which the boy was holding in reserve.

"Chappy, this is my friend Whitney."

"Hi," he said without even looking at her.

"Push us both." Robin sat down. "You get on top, Whitney."

"Nah. I'll swing myself."

"C'mon. Don't be a party pooper."

"Every party has a pooper, that's why I invited you . . ." Chappy started singing.

"You keep quiet," Robin ordered.

Whitney slipped one foot onto the seat beside Robin, then the other one.

"Okay, Chaps, push us." Slowly they rose into the air, farther back and farther forward, until the chains slackened and snapped taut at the break of each swing. "Harder, harder. Push harder." Whitney and Robin lifted, then banged onto the swing, Robin screaming, "Ow, ow, ow," then laughing, then screaming, "Higher, higher," until Chappy was barely touching the swing bottom with his fingertips.

"Don't stop!" Robin shrieked.

Whitney looked back, but Chappy, in a tired heap,

didn't move or speak as they descended, slowed down, were gliding now.

"Chappy, stop us," Robin insisted.

The heap rose and caught the swing from behind Whitney, pitching her forward, Robin backward. Whitney threw herself into a forward roll, leaving Robin whimpering on her back behind her. Chappy ran to Robin. "You all right?" He lifted her to her feet.

Robin groaned. Whitney hoisted herself to her feet and brushed the gravel off her pants.

"You're crazy, you know that?" Chappy brushed off Robin's back.

"I'm perfectly all right." Robin pushed him away. "Did you get hurt?"

Whitney shook her head.

"You want to spend the night at my house tonight?"

"Sure," she said, wondering now why earlier she had felt sore at Robin.

"Look, I gotta go," Chappy interrupted. "You gonna watch us practice, or what?"

Robin turned to Whitney. "Let's watch for a while. Maybe they'll let us play."

"Nah."

"Why not?"

"I don't feel like it."

"C'mon, Whitney, at least until your mother comes. There's nothing else to do."

Whitney sat.

"If you change your mind," Robin called over her shoulder, "I'll be on the bleachers."

I won't, Whitney said to herself, pumping hard to get the swing going. After a while, out of the corner of her eye, she saw her mother's white Ford convertible creeping down Lawrence Avenue.

"Whitney Bennett, where's your coat?" her mother wanted to know as soon as Whitney had jumped into the front seat and slammed the door.

Whitney looked down at herself; she had forgotten all about her coat. "It's in the gym," she muttered. "I'll bring it home tomorrow."

"And where's Robin?"

"Robin?" Whitney slouched down in her seat. "I don't know."

"Well, go fetch her. And find your coat. You're going to catch pneumonia dressed like that."

Whitney ran back across the parking lot. It had begun to rain but she didn't care. She found Robin under the bleachers with Chappy. "My mother's waiting."

"Where've you been? Chappy says you're real cute."

Whitney scowled.

"Isn't that right, Chappy?" Chappy shuffled his feet and nodded, smiling vaguely at Whitney.

Whitney wanted to kick him. "Let's go." She tugged on Robin's sleeve.

"What's the rush?"

"My mother's in a hurry."

"But I don't want to go home yet. It's early."

"My ma'll give you a lift," Chappy offered.

"Really? That's sweet."

Releasing Robin's sweatshirt sleeve, Whitney started back toward the school alone.

"Hey, Whitney. Wait. I've got something for you. Stay right here," Robin said to Chappy, "and don't move an inch." She hooked her arm through Whitney's, pulling her back inside to the gym. "Here." She took a brown paper bag out of her coat pocket and handed it to Whitney. "Don't open it till you get home and don't tell anyone."

Whitney reached into the bag.

Robin snatched her hand out. "No, you have to promise, not until you get home or I'll take it back."

Whitney dropped her hand to her side.

Robin ushered her back outside. "Isn't he adorable?" she whispered into Whitney's curls. "He was the most popular boy in Grant School last year." Then she was off again.

Whitney didn't speak to her mother all the way home except to say yes or no or grunt that she didn't know. Her mother finally asked her why she never told her anything about what she was doing and what in the world was she doing that she had to be so secretive? Whitney said she was just tired, that was all, and what was for dinner? Liver was for dinner, which made her want to throw up.

At home Whitney ran upstairs to her room and flung

herself across her bed. Halfheartedly she emptied Robin's brown paper bag; a small white box fell on the spread. Inside, between two pads of cotton, was a shiny silver ring with two rows of tiny linked hearts engraved around the band. Thrilled, she slipped the ring down her right pinky — it hung loose — then on her fourth finger, then on her other fourth finger. It didn't look right anywhere, and why did it feel so uncomfortable? She remembered Robin's invitation to spend the night, saw Chappy and Robin huddled under the bleachers, heard Robin say, "Oh, how sweet," or "How very sweet of your mother" — just the way Charlotte talked. She worked the ring back over her knuckle and threw it across the room, hating it now. Then she hated herself for being ungrateful.

The next thing she knew her mother was shaking her awake and telling her to wash up, comb her hair, and come downstairs for dinner; everyone was waiting for her. As soon as her mother was safely down the hallway Whitney retrieved the ring and buried it in the bureau drawer under her underwear. She started down the stairs, then stopped when she remembered what was for dinner.

"Whitney, is that you?" her mother called from the dining room.

"Uh huh."

"Well, hurry up, your food's getting cold."

Whitney slid silently down the banister, which she was forbidden to do, and dropped into her chair. Her mother eyed her suspiciously, but to her surprise didn't ask any more questions about Robin or the tryouts. And for some strange reason, Whitney didn't dare ask why, her mother had cooked, just for her, a cheeseburger with fried onions and her favorite vegetable, spinach with cream sauce.

CHAPTER FIVE

Geography Class

Whitney slipped into her seat in geography class, barely containing her excitement about the present she had secretly been toting around all morning. When the bell rang she had an impulse to thrust it at Robin with just enough time to say "Here" and be done with it, but once again her shyness got the better of her. The ring was exactly like the one Robin had given her except it had clover etched around the edges and she had paid fifty cents extra to have Robin's initials engraved on the inside of the band.

Robin was pulling shoestring licorice out of her partially opened desk when Whitney reached across the aisle and discreetly slipped the beautifully wrapped package into her desk. Robin bit away the piece of licorice she was working on, let the rest slither back down into the compartment, and lowered the desk top on her forearms. The crackling of wrapping paper was starting to attract attention. Whitney felt more nervous than ever. Pangs of doubt were quickly turning to regret that she hadn't found something better, more special, less copycattish, when Mr. Palmer, who was touching various parts of a sphere with a pointer and asking unintelligible questions, suddenly bellowed "Robin!" and scared both her and Robin out of their seats.

"Yes, sir." Robin tried to ease her hands out without letting the desk lid bang.

"Answer the question."

"Excuse me, I didn't quite get the question."

Mr. Palmer was standing over her. "You didn't quite get the question because you weren't quite listening."

Robin bit her lips, tried to look contrite.

"The question was, young lady, how many poles are there?"

"Four." Robin smiled hopefully. Whitney cringed.

"Oh, yes? And what are they, my intelligent little bird?"

"North, south, east, and west." Robin was grinning, her tongue red with licorice.

Mr. Palmer was chewing on his lips now, Whitney thought because he was mad. "Whitney." Whitney slipped down in her seat. "Don't sink, Miss Bennett, rise up. Help your friend out of this jam . . . Well?"

"Yes, sir?" Whitney barely whispered.

"The correct answer, Whitney. What is the correct answer to that question?"

Whitney felt so flustered now that she couldn't remember the question.

"Are you there, Whitney?"

Whitney nodded. "Two," she blurted out, which seemed like the right answer, though she still couldn't think to what.

"Ah, very good. Why must you look so crestfallen?" Whitney's face got hotter, her eyes started watering. Mr. Palmer backed up the aisle. "Yes, boys and girls, as you all should know by this time in your educational development, there are two poles. As a reward for that little demonstration of brilliance, Miss Bennett, you may choose your project first from the list on the board. Then we will proceed around the room and conclude last but not least with our bright star, Miss Wheeler."

Whitney looked toward Robin for a cue, a sign, but Robin was busy writing in her notebook.

Whitney chose Switzerland, then Mr. Palmer went around the room. When the far rows were having their turns, Robin shut her notebook, opened her lunch bag which was now in her lap, lifted her desk top all the way up, and began munching on a chicken leg behind the lid. She finished it quietly and swiftly, then attacked a wing. Suddenly Mr. Palmer shifted back across the room to Tommy Jensen at the head of Robin's row. Robin stayed under cover until Mr. Palmer turned to write Tommy's name on the board next to the Congo, then she pulled her notebook back out and reopened it, her head cocked, the tip of her pen poised between her lips. She was working feverishly when Mr. Palmer called on her. Whitney strained to see what she was writing but couldn't make it out.

Robin squinted at the board. "There's nothing left."

"How observant. What do you suggest we do?"

Robin shrugged. "I guess I don't have to do a project." Someone snickered.

Mr. Palmer headed down the aisle toward her. Robin opened her legs. The lunch bag dropped between them into the folds of her skirt. She eased her notebook shut and, just before he reached her, clasped her hands together on her desk top. Mr. Palmer looked mean and angry now. Robin's grin faded. He grabbed her desk lid. It opened with such force that one of the hinges snapped. "Chicken bones," he cried. "She leaves chicken bones behind for us to remember her by." Everyone in the class roared. "Quiet!" Mr. Palmer whirled around. Everyone faced forward, hands folded. "Miss Wheeler, is this the way you're accustomed to behaving in all your classes?"

"I was hungry." The class burst out laughing again.

"Enough! Go to the board, Miss Wheeler."

Robin didn't budge.

"I *said*, GO TO THE BOARD!" He pointed to the front of the room.

Robin stood slowly, her eyes on Mr. Palmer. The lunch bag dropped to the floor. Robin slipped between Mr. Palmer and the row of desks, stepping over her lunch.

"PICK IT UP!" he bellowed.

Robin halted, turned, picked up her lunch, stood at attention.

"To THE BOARD," he barked over her head.

Robin saluted, turned again, marched to the front of the room. More suppressed giggles. Mr. Palmer surveyed the class, his face sterner than ever. The room was silent. "The clean one, Miss Wheeler." Robin sidled to the right, lunch bag clutched in hand. "Take this down: 'I promise never to leave chicken bones in my geography class desk again. It is unsanitary, unladylike, and un-c-o-u-t-h. Furthermore, I will never eat in geography class unless I have enough for everyone.' "

Robin copied frantically. Her handwriting was beautiful.

"Very good, Miss Wheeler."

Robin put the chalk in the holder and was heading back to her seat.

"Did I say you could sit down?"

Robin stopped at the head of her row, the lunch bag hidden now behind her back.

Mr. Palmer seemed to be smiling, but the smile went away when the class started murmuring again. "Good show, Miss Wheeler, but you're not done yet. During lunch today you will write that promise one hundred times on these boards. The rest of the class is dismissed for a head start on the lunch lines."

There were whoops and shouts as those up front lunged for the door. Whitney stacked her books to leave, then she noticed Robin gazing forlornly at her. She slid back into her seat. Robin smiled gratefully.

"You may leave as well, Miss Bennett."

Whitney glanced at her friend. "Is it all right if I stay?"

"May I ask why you're so eager to miss your lunch?"

"Because . . ." Whitney felt responsible too but couldn't explain why. She shrugged her shoulders, stared at the floor.

"You're like Siamese twins, you two. Or more like the North Pole and the South Pole. Start writing, Miss Wheeler."

The chalk screeched. It hurt Whitney's sensitive chewing spots, which made her realize how hungry she was for her bologna sandwich. Mr. Palmer sat on the desk top in front of Whitney, one foot perched on the empty chair. "Why do you brood so much, Miss Bennett?"

Whitney's eyes darted around the room, looking for something to focus on.

"Don't be scared, I won't bite you."

Robin giggled.

"And you, Miss Wheeler-dealer, can't you ever take anything seriously?" Mr. Palmer winked at Whitney. "Do you think she'll try to eat her chicken in here again tomorrow?"

Whitney glanced at Robin. She didn't know whether to answer or not. "I passed her something during class," she blurted out, feeling overwhelmed by guilt.

Mr. Palmer raised an eyebrow. "The chicken?"

"N-no."

"Do you want to write on the board too? Is that what you're trying to tell me?"

Whitney shook her head. Her handwriting was terrible, and sometimes when she was asked to write on the board she couldn't even make her hand form the letters legibly.

"Give me your notebook."

Whitney's hand shook as she gave up her geography notebook for inspection. Mr. Palmer opened it, balanced it on his knee, jotted something down. "Want to go for a walk?" He tore the sheet out and folded it.

Whitney nodded.

"Take this note to the teachers' lunchroom." He pulled his wallet out of his pocket. "And get me a hot plate. If they give you a hard time, show your note. What do you kids usually have with your lunches?"

"Milk."

"And ice cream," Robin piped up from the board.

"Who asked you? Keep writing. And milk and ice cream for all of us," he whispered in Whitney's ear, tucking a five-dollar bill into her fist. "Scram."

When Whitney returned with the food, Mr. Palmer dismissed Robin from her punishment and they ate at their desks. Robin opened her present, though Whitney was embarrassed and begged her not to, but Mr. Palmer insisted too so it was a losing battle. He admired the ring, which Robin slipped right on without even noticing the engraved initials. Then he asked them if they didn't have boyfriends. Robin said of course she did but she wouldn't tell him who, and Whitney said she did too, feeling ashamed now of the ring and wishing Mr. Palmer knew Robin had already given her one.

"I can see I'm not going to get anywhere with you two. Go on, get out of here. Wait. Throw away your garbage. You can take your ice cream with you."

Robin dropped her lunch bag in the basket next to Mr. Palmer's desk while Whitney stood holding the classroom door.

"And don't forget to bring your assignments in tomorrow."

Robin curtsied. "Yes, Mr. Palmer." Then she turned and ran.

"And if you want to make yourselves useful," he shouted after her, "you can come back after school and water my plants."

They slammed the door and ran down the hall arm in arm, giggling nervously, then burst out laughing at the girls' room door.

CHAPTER SIX

Alone

Whitney got out of the car and slammed the door. From the curb she watched the Wheelers' station wagon disappear down the street. Her own house was deserted; there wasn't even a note. Rarely did she have the house to herself; it would be a good time to check up on her stash. She was pulling up the loose floorboard in the basement when she thought she heard the car motor. Dizzy with fear, she stomped on the board to force it back. A long splinter caught on the edge of the neighboring board. She ripped the splinter loose; the board fell neatly into place, except now there was a quarter-inch crack where the splinter had been. Then she thought she heard a car door slam. She dropped the extra piece of wood and ran up the stairs to the landing. The house was dead; she peeked out the window — the driveway was empty. Back downstairs she fit the splinter in place. It still didn't look right. She opened up the floor again, threw the splinter in, and lowered the board. That would have to do. The phone rang. She froze against the wall. Should she answer it or not? She started for the basement extension but then ran upstairs to the kitchen phone.

"Hello, Whitney. Where are you, dear?"

"In the kitchen."

"I just called you at Robin's. Are you all right?"

"Uh huh."

"What're you doing?"

"Homework."

"Have you had lunch?"

Whitney mumbled no.

"There's vegetable soup in the refrigerator, and crackers. The cake on the counter is for company tomorrow night. You haven't had some already, have you?"

"No."

"Well, don't. Your father had some extra work to do at the office and I'm out at Fabric Land." Whitney was silent. "You'll be home later?"

"Uh huh."

"Bye, dear."

Whitney hung up, went to the refrigerator, and stared at all the filmy containers, everything neatly packaged and obscured except a tray of chicken soaking in a black sauce. She slammed the door in disgust. Soup! As if she were sick or something. She dragged up to her room, threw her coat across the bed. Lady jumped on the bed and pawed her coat. At her desk Whitney opened her notebook to English and some sentence diagramming she had started in study hall, then she stretched out beside Lady.

It had begun to snow, and the snow made her want to call Robin. If it stuck maybe she would call her. They could meet halfway for a snowball fight.

Whitney glanced out the window. The trees were covered now, the brown earth disappearing under the white powdery stuff. She got back up. Lady abandoned her spot, followed Whitney into her parents' bedroom and stood by her feet while she dialed. "Robin? Want to take the dogs to the park? I'll meet you halfway on Mountain, then we'll —"

"Can't."

"Why not?"

"Chappy's here."

They were silent. Whitney swallowed her pride. "Well, how about later on, after he leaves?"

"We're going to the Rialto. Gee, Whitney," she whispered, "if you could get someone to ask you out, we could double date."

"Like who?" she snarled.

"I could ask Chappy if he knows —"

"Chappy!" Whitney banged down the receiver, then stood there for a long time waiting for it to ring back. But she was the one who had hung up. She could call back, ask Robin why she had hung up like that, then say they must've gotten disconnected. But then what? Double date? Ha! Fat chance. Robin had just said that to rub it in. Anyway, who wanted to go on a dumb date with a couple of idiotic boys? Not her. She stared at the phone, angry with herself for having called in the first place. She certainly didn't need to be with anybody to have a good time.

She leashed Lady and walked the mile to the park alone. It was snowing harder now. By the time she reached the stream that fed into the lake, an inch had accumulated; the wind had made a drift around the trunk of the Swiss tree. She let herself fall backwards into the drift. Lady leapt in beside her. "Hey." She gave her a shove. "You're messing up my angel." Lady whimpered, nosing at the edge of the drift. Whitney threw her arms around her dog's neck. When she let go, Lady sprang free and ran around in circles, chasing her tail. Whitney kicked snow at her, and Lady leapt into the air, snapping at it, her body gyrating as she fell back to the ground. Whitney lunged for her, grabbed her around the middle, and they rolled in the snow, first one on top, then the other, until Whitney was soaked through. The wind felt bitter now, the snow wet and cold. She snapped Lady back on the leash. They headed home. A single car passed them on Mountain Avenue, the snow so thick and swirling that Whitney could barely make out the houses set far back from the road. She paused at Sherwood Parkway, then decided to take the long way around, past Robin's house and back to Mountain Avenue.

The station wagon was in the driveway. Maybe Robin

was home from the movies already... There was still time for a walk before it got dark. The streetlamps came on. Whitney started up the front walk, stopped. But maybe *he* had come back home with her. Her tracks reached the front porch. Eager to go inside, Lady whined and tugged on the leash. And if he *was* there, she'd be sent away... Whitney shuddered and yanked Lady back to the street. She turned, for a moment watched their tracks filling, then pushed against the wind and blinding snow to Charlotte's house across the street.

Charlotte's mother answered the door. Whitney would have to leave the dog outside, she said. Charlotte appeared then in some sort of filmy gown, and her mother left. No, Charlotte wouldn't come out. It was too cold, and anyway, she hated the snow. She suggested they lock Lady in the garage so Whitney could come in.

"No, thanks." Whitney backed down the stairs.

"Hey, Whitney. Come back tomorrow afternoon without your dog. I'll teach you how to play bridge. I just learned."

Whitney walked backwards a few more steps. "Sure. I'll do that."

"Maybe you could even stay for dinner. I'll ask my mother."

"No, don't."

"Why not? It'll be just like old times."

Suddenly Muffin, crouched between Charlotte's legs, leapt out onto the porch. Lady lunged forward, ripping the leash out of Whitney's mitten. "Get him away, get him away!" Charlotte squealed, jumping up and down on the doorsill.

Its back arched, the cat hissed at Lady, who was inching toward it, then took a swipe at Lady's nose. Lady yowled. Whitney grabbed her by the scruff of her neck. Charlotte stopped screaming, tiptoed through the snow in her slippers, scooped up her cat, and stroking down its raised fur and kissing it all over she retreated inside, slamming the door.

"Next time, leave that beast at home," Charlotte called through the letter slot in the door as Whitney dragged Lady off the stoop.

"She's not a beast," Whitney shouted back, but the metal slot had clattered shut.

The snow came up over the tops of her shoes now. She kicked through it, letting it seep down her socks, and when she and Lady arrived home she felt chilled to her bones. She tried to sneak past her mother, who was playing the piano in the living room, but when Whitney reached the stairs her mother spied her out of the corner of her eye.

"Whitney Bennett, where have you been?" The music stopped.

"Out playing," Whitney mumbled.

"In this weather, without your boots?"

"What song was that?" Whitney asked to change the subject.

"Come here." Her mother lowered the keyboard cover.

"When are you ever going to learn to take proper care of yourself?" She stripped off Whitney's wet things, then gave her a pat on her bottom. "Now go put on dry clothes this instant. You're going to catch your death."

Whitney ran up to her room, Lady at her heels. She put on her old green corduroys which she had outgrown and an orange pullover. The colors didn't go together, she knew, but she liked them. Her father was shut up in the bedroom — she could hear him snoring. She'd have to use the basement phone. She tiptoed downstairs and got past her mother, who was peering into the pots and pans cupboard in the kitchen. She was halfway down the basement stairs before her mother stopped her. "Is that you, Whitney?"

"Yeah."

"Did you put on dry clothes?"

"Yeah."

"What're you doing now?"

"Watching TV."

"Why don't you watch it up here?"

"Too noisy."

Whitney waited. Pans clattered. She went the rest of the way down, turned on the TV, and waited a few more minutes, staring at the screen, before she finally picked up the phone and dialed. "Robin?"

"Can't talk now." The voice was breathless. "Chappy and I are right in the middle of a TV program."

"Wait. You want to go sledding tomorrow?"

"I'll call you later."

The phone clicked in Whitney's ear. Whitney held the receiver until she noticed her mother leaning over the banister staring at her. Casually she laid it in its cradle.

"Who were you calling?"

Whitney shrugged. "No one."

"You were talking to no one?"

"I was going to call Robin but I changed my mind."

"You two see too much of each other. You should spread the wealth a little."

"What wealth?"

"Don't be difficult, Whitney. You know what I mean. Why don't you give Charlotte a ring?"

"Charlotte's a drag."

"I'm sure there are plenty of nice girls in your class you could spend an afternoon with."

Whitney stared at the TV screen.

"What about that pretty blonde girl down the street?"

"Aw, Ma." Whitney wrapped her arms around her ankles, balanced her chin on her knee. "Can't I watch the end of this show?"

"Of course you can." Her mother started back up the stairs.

Maybe they were watching the same program. Maybe they were doing other things and pretending to watch.

"But, Whitney?"

Whitney raised her chin.

"Change those pants before dinner. They're way too tight on you and they look ghastly with that sweater."

Whitney squeezed her legs to her chest and rocked.

Her mother's heels clicked up the remainder of the stairs; now they were tapping over her head on the kitchen linoleum. She opened her mouth and hollered at the top of her lungs, "I look ghastly no matter what I wear."

"That's not true, dear," her mother called back. "If you'd listen to me every once in a while and pay a little attention to the way you look, you could compete with the best of them." Her mother's voice was cheerful, even hopeful.

Whitney pressed the on-off button with her foot. "What's for dinner?" she yelled up again.

"None of your business, but come change your clothes, it'll be ready soon."

On the way through the kitchen Whitney lifted the lid off the heating pot.

"It's Welsh rarebit." Her mother snatched the lid away. "And I don't want to hear a single complaint out of you."

"I'm starved, Ma. Can't we have something else?"

"It won't hurt you to eat a light meal once in a while. Now go put those pants in the ragbag, and while you're up there call your father."

"Can I at least eat downstairs?"

"No."

"I want to see the end of the movie."

"Ask your father."

Upstairs she shook her father out of his nap. "Dinner's ready."

He grunted, rolled over.

"Can I eat in the basement and watch TV?"

"Why?" He rolled back. "We're not good enough company for you?"

"Pleeease."

"Stop whining. There'll be plenty of time after dinner for TV. Now get out of here so I can dress."

Whitney slammed his bedroom door. She could never do anything she wanted. She'd eat with them all right, but she wouldn't answer anybody or even look at anybody. No one. And she never wanted to see Robin again. Why had she gone and called her? How could she be so stupid? She put on her new brown wool pants which itched her and made her look as big as a house. Her mother yelled at her to hurry up. When she dragged downstairs into the dining room, her parents were both seated at the table waiting.

"Whitney?"

Whitney glared at her mother.

"Say the grace, please, dear."

Whitney stared at the pool of cheese on her plate while she recited the prayer.

"Thank you, dear. Pass the salad to your father, please."

Whitney reached for the salad without looking up and dropped it down on her other side.

"What's eating you?" Her father dipped into the bowl of greens.

"I hate Welsh rarebit."

Her father stopped serving himself. "Apologize to your mother."

Whitney kept her eyes on her plate. "No."

"Don't get fresh with me, young lady."

"Well, why *can't* I eat downstairs?"

"And stop that whining." Her father was yelling now.

Whitney threw her fork down on the table and was already pushing her chair out to leave when her father ordered her up to her room. "And when you've learned some manners," he shouted after her, "you can come back down."

But she had already decided she would never come back down. She lay on her bed for a long time holding onto her growling stomach and feeling sorry for herself. Even Lady had stayed downstairs, more interested in the food than in her. Finally she started reading the latest book she had gotten from the library, about a boy who becomes a veterinarian. As soon as she had decided *she* wanted to be a veterinarian, Robin had said that's what she wanted to be too, the dirty copycat. Well, Whitney didn't want to be a veterinarian anymore. It was childish, and these books were babyish and phony.

There was a knock on her door. She turned to face the wall. The door opened, and her mother walked gingerly over to the edge of her bed. "I brought you a sandwich and milk."

Whitney was still.

"Turn over, dear."

Whitney propped herself up, took the plate and glass.

"Is something the matter?"

"No."

"Something you're keeping from us?"

"Nothing's the matter. I'm *fine*."

"All right, don't get all worked up."

Whitney took a bite out of the ham sandwich. It was hard to swallow. She rubbed her eyes with her fist.

"Well, I'll leave you alone so you can read."

Whitney turned her back to her mother and stared out the window.

"Isn't the snow lovely?"

Whitney nodded.

"When I was a girl I loved the snow . . ."

Whitney could feel her mother's eyes on her back.

"There was a window seat in my room and I used to watch the cornstalks disappear."

Whitney swallowed the lump in her throat.

"Can I get you anything else?" Her mother stood.

Whitney shook her head no.

"Please look at me, Whitney," her mother pleaded from the doorway.

Whitney turned over to face her mother but stared at the floor. Her mother was still waiting silently, Whitney knew, for her to obey. "Thanks for the sandwich," she mumbled, hoping that would be enough.

Her mother sighed before she disappeared into the hallway.

"Shut the door, will you, Ma?"

Her mother peeked back in. "Anything you want, dear." She eased the door to until it was cracked.

"All the way, Ma."

The latch clicked in place. Tears dropped out of Whitney's eyes onto the sandwich. She had been fine until her mother came in. Why didn't they leave her alone? Robin's parents let her do whatever she felt like doing. But she hated Robin too, she reminded herself, and she wasn't going to call her up, not tomorrow or the next day or the next, even if it meant she never spoke to her again. After all, Robin was already interested in someone else.

Whitney bit into the soggy bread. The juices in her mouth started to flow. She gobbled up the rest of the sandwich, gulped down the milk. Her stomach cried for more. Perhaps the phone would ring . . . but it was already getting late. Anyway, didn't she have better things to do with her time than wait around for Robin to call? Well, when Robin did call, she would make sure she wasn't around. Then Robin would be sorry. She'd see how it felt, for a change.

CHAPTER SEVEN

The Fight

Early the next morning when the phone rang, Whitney leapt out of bed, pressed her ear to the door, then ran downstairs and grabbed the phone off the kitchen wall. "I got it, Ma," she shouted into the receiver. The extension clicked. "Robin?"

"It's me, Charlotte."

"Oh, Charlotte."

"I'm having a bridge party this afternoon. Want to come?"

"I've got to go to Sunday school."

"It's not till two."

"Well, maybe."

"Yes or no."

"I'll have to ask my mother. I'll call you back." Whitney glanced out the kitchen window after she hung up.

Snow blanketed the yard. The trees, laden with ice, glistened in the sun. What a day for Sunday school! She called Charlotte back to ask her if she wanted to go sledding instead.

"It's too cold," Charlotte complained. "You coming?"

"I haven't asked yet."

"Whitney, if you can go sledding, you can come over."

"I'll call you right back." She hung up again, picked up the receiver, dialed. No answer.

"Feeling better this morning?" Whitney's mother stood in the kitchen doorway, knotting the sash around her robe. Whitney grunted as she jumped off the stool under the phone. "What did Charlotte want?"

"She's having a bridge party."

"A bridge party? Aren't you girls a little young for that sort of thing?"

"What's age got to do with it?" Whitney walked to the sink, gazed out the window.

"Excuse me for asking." Her mother took silverware out of the drawer. "So when is this grown-up event?"

"This afternoon."

"Are you going?" Mrs. Bennett began setting the kitchen table with great deliberation, as if she really wasn't very interested in her daughter's plans.

"What's for breakfast?"

"Hotcakes and sausage, your favorite." Her mother ran a stream of hot water over a can of frozen orange juice. "You should go." She pulled ingredients off the lazy Susan in the cupboard. "It'll do you good."

"I want to be outside today." Whitney hesitated. "Can I skip Sunday school?"

Her mother looked up from her sifting.

"Please, just this once."

"It's a bad habit to get into."

"Dad never goes to church."

"All right. If you go to the party."

"Thanks, Ma." She dialed Charlotte. At least something was going right. "Hi, it's me again. I'm coming."

"I already have a foursome."

"What do you mean?"

"I mean I don't need you anymore."

"Okay, bye." Whitney's voice drifted off.

"So?" Her mother poured water over the sausages.

"Nothing."

"What time are you due?"

"Two."

"Why so glum? You've got the whole morning. Go get dressed. And wake your father. Breakfast will be ready in ten minutes."

Whitney peeked in at her father. She was staring at him when he opened one eye. Suddenly Whitney felt tongue-tied — as if she'd just been caught at something.

"What do you want?" He pulled the sheet up to his chest.

"Breakfast'll be ready in ten minutes. You're supposed to get up."

"I am, am I?"

"Yeah, Ma says."

"Well, stop gaping, shut the door, and maybe I will."

Whitney slammed the door. Her father was always grumpy when he was wakened, and she always seemed to get stuck with waking him. But it wasn't her fault he had to get up. She had to be extra careful this morning not to rub him the wrong way or she'd end up at church. She shut herself in her room, put on two layers of warm clothes, and went back downstairs to the kitchen. Her mother was tending the hotcakes. Whitney brought her plate to the stove and was served two sausage links and a stack of cakes. Whitney drowned her cakes in maple syrup. She felt her mother's eyes on her and glanced up. "Some of it's for my next round," she explained.

Her mother shook her head and sighed.

"I've got another round coming, haven't I?"

"Yes, it's fine if you actually save it. It just doesn't look good."

"What difference does it make how it looks?"

"Don't start in," her mother warned, "or I'll send you to Sunday school and take you to the service afterwards."

"Do what your mother says," her father ordered as he entered the kitchen. "Understand?" Whitney nodded. "Let's all have a peaceful meal for a change."

Mrs. Bennett set his breakfast in front of him. He opened the Sunday *Times*. Whitney handed him the syrup pitcher, then watched him pour until syrup ran off his cakes into a thick pool around the edges. He cleared his throat, rattled the paper as he folded and adjusted it, and took one last look around the table before he disappeared behind the front page.

"May I be excused?" Whitney laid her knife and fork across her plate.

"You didn't finish."

Whitney wolfed down the last two cakes. "*Now* may I be excused?"

Her mother nodded vaguely.

Whitney went back upstairs to her parents' room to try Robin again. Still no answer. Where was she? Nine, ten . . . Why didn't she answer the phone? Fourteen, fifteen . . . Whitney banged down the receiver and had gone to change her pants for the second time when her father knocked on her door. "Open up."

"Just a minute, I'm dressing." She zipped up her pants before she opened the door.

"How about helping me shovel the driveway?"

"Really?" Whitney gathered her clothes up off the floor, unable to believe her ears. "Sure."

"Come on, then. You can use the small aluminum shovel." He went down the hall.

Whitney smiled. She loved to work with her father, but usually she was only allowed to do little chores. More often she was told a chore was a man's job and she'd be in the way. She could rake leaves, but she couldn't use the power mower. She could weed the garden, but she couldn't help him dig the plots or fertilize.

She could wash windows and screens, but she wasn't allowed to climb the ladder with him and put them up. She could sweep, but she couldn't shovel — that is, until the last snowfall, when she had taken matters into her own hands, gotten up early, and had the entire front walk done by the time her parents got up. Although her father hadn't said anything, she'd surprised him all right.

She stood at attention on the front porch, waiting for orders. He pointed to a narrower version of his shovel leaning against the house. "You start back at the garage and we'll meet . . . in the middle."

Balancing the shovel against her shoulder the way her father did, Whitney plodded through the snow, Lady bounding in and out through the drifts beside her. Her arms started to ache long before she had even reached the corner of the house, but she kept forcing herself to pick up the heavy stuff, eager to prove she could do as much as he could. When they met, she could hardly keep the snow on the shovel. She backtracked over her territory to clear the cave-ins, heaving the snow far into the yard. For a few moments all her strength came back as her father blew on his knuckles and watched. "That'll do, Whitney," he called out.

Whitney leaned on her shovel, panting, and tried to catch her breath. She was sweating all over and freezing at the same time.

"You think you can handle the porch while I do the walkways?"

"Sure."

"You're not too tired?" He put his arm around her shoulders.

"Tired?" She made a face. "Not me. Want me to help with the sidewalk too?"

"Do the porch. Then we'll see."

They parted at the walkway. Whitney was able to push most of the snow off the porch and steps into the bushes. When she began the sidewalk, she realized she could barely lift the shovel anymore, at least not with very much on it. She was about to redouble her efforts when her father came back up the driveway. "You're making extra work for yourself," he said as he scooped a large shovelful of snow off the flagstones. "All we need here is a narrow footpath." He quickly cleared his way through to her as she stood watching. "Oh, my God." He seemed to be staring at the porch. "What did you do that for?"

"What?"

"The azaleas — you've crushed them." He began knocking the loose stuff off the tops of the bagged bushes. "You have to think about what you're doing, Whitney. I can't be hanging over your shoulder every single minute. There." He brushed away the last of the snow. "What's the matter?" He pounded his gloves together. "You pooped?"

"No."

"Give me your shovel. I'll take it back to the garage."

"I can do it." Whitney clung to her shovel.

"All right. Take mine too."

She dragged both shovels behind her, feeling deflated, then kicked the back tire of the car and dragged herself into the house. Her father stood by the kitchen radiator warming his hands. Whitney sat on the landing step, her back to him.

"Did I work you too hard?"

"Aw, Dad." She kicked off her boots.

"You're a good worker. I was glad to have your help."

She felt a surge of pleasure. "It was nothing." She unbuttoned her coat.

"I'll give you a tip though for the future."

She shook out her wet things over the rug.

"Take it a little slower, a little easier next time, and you won't tire so quickly."

It may have been good advice but it sounded to her like criticism. "I'm *not* tired." She pouted.

"All right, all right. Learn the hard way."

She made a wide circle around him. She could barely hang up her coat. Still in her clothes, she crawled under the covers of her bed and curled up in a ball. Outside her window it was gray again, gray and white and gloomy. She hadn't even noticed that it had clouded over while she was shoveling. Snowflakes so large she could see the designs in them floated past her window. She took off her glasses to rest her eyes for a minute, and the next thing she knew her mother was shaking her. It was one-thirty. She shouldn't be late for Charlotte's get-together, her mother said.

"Will you drive me?" she asked, forgetting for a moment she'd been uninvited.

"The roads are dangerous."

"I'm too tired to go." She groped around the bed for her glasses.

"It's not a long walk. I'll heat up a bowl of soup for you."

The soup tasted good but it wasn't enough. She left the house hungry. The porch was nearly covered again; the gravel in the driveway had completely disappeared. Whitney scraped the steps clean with her feet. The flakes were smaller and harder now, falling steadily and silently. There was no wind; the air was warmer. On Mountain Avenue she started catching snowflakes in her mouth. Out here it felt good to be alive. She let out a whoop. The sound got swallowed up somehow by the heaviness, the whiteness, the stillness.

When she got to Charlotte's house she did a sudden about-face. Across the street she rang Robin's bell. Robin loved snow too, just the way she did. They could have a snowball fight, then maybe build a fort — it was good packing snow.

Mr. Wheeler opened the door. "Hiya, kiddo, you're just in time for dessert. Come on in."

Once inside, Whitney peered into the dining room. Mrs. Wheeler smiled at her. "Sit down, Whitney. Take Robin's seat. I'll cut another slice of cake."

Whitney's mouth watered. "Thanks. Where's Robin?"

"Across the street."

"Across the street?"

"At Charlotte's. Sit."

But of course. Why hadn't she thought of that? What in the world had made her believe Robin would be right here waiting for her? Whitney backed into the vestibule.

"Don't be shy." Mr. Wheeler put his arm around her shoulders, urging her back to the dining room. "Since when have you turned down a piece of cake?" He squeezed her around the waist. "Besides, I need a girl with me at my Sunday meal. My own daughter's deserted me." He pulled off her hat.

"No, please." Whitney snatched it back. "I want to be outdoors, you know, while it's still snowing."

"All right for you, Whitney. You don't know what a treat you're missing." He patted his stomach. "How about a slice for the road?"

Whitney shook her head.

"Go on," he called after her as he sat back down. "Abandon me, just like your friend did."

Whitney opened the door.

"Enjoy your walk," Mrs. Wheeler called out. "And don't mind him. He's harmless."

Whitney closed the door noiselessly. Now what? Charlotte's? They would have to let her in. Robin hadn't told her she was going, hadn't even called her, in fact. The snow pressed in around her, bent her over. Given the choice, Robin would never sit cooped up inside on a snowy afternoon playing a dumb game of cards. Given the choice . . . given the choice . . . Whitney tried to stand up straight and smile when Charlotte's door opened. Mrs. Harrison looked suspiciously around and behind her for her dog before she invited her in. Whitney stepped up on the doorsill. "Is Robin here?"

"Yes, she is, but do come all the way in so I can shut out the cold."

Whitney stepped back down. "That's all right. I'll wait out here."

Next Robin opened the door. "Hiya, Whitney, come on in. Charlotte says it's okay."

Whitney stood her ground. "How come you didn't call me?"

"I did call you."

"You did not."

"I did too. Ask your mother."

"All right, I will." Each stood glaring at the other. Whitney waited to be coaxed inside again but Robin said nothing. "Want to come for a walk?" Whitney finally asked lamely.

"Can't. Charlotte'll get mad."

"So?"

"Whitney!" Robin stepped back up onto the doorsill. "First I'm supposed to call you night and day, now I'm supposed to leave in the middle of a party just because you feel like — "

"I thought you said you *did* call."

"Well, what if I didn't? What's the big deal?"

"You *said* you would."

"I have other things to do in my life, Whitney Gabriel

Bennett, besides call you up every single minute of every single day."

"Who asked you to? Just because some stupid boy's taken you to a lousy movie, all of a sudden you think you're hot stuff."

"You're jealous."

"I am not."

"You are too. Even Charlotte says so."

"Charlotte!" Whitney leapt off the porch.

"Whitney?"

"What?" Whitney picked up some snow, packed it, hurled it at a tree, missed.

"Don't be mad."

"I'm not." She packed another one, hurled that, missed again.

"I can't help it if everyone wants to be with me. You're not the only person in the world, you know, and even Charlotte hasn't ever been *treated* to a movie."

"In that case," Whitney snarled, fighting back her tears, "you sure don't need me." She pulled off her mitten and wriggled the ring off her finger.

Robin squinted at it, held now in suspension between Whitney's pinky and thumb. Their eyes met. Whitney threw it on the stoop. "Take it. It doesn't fit right anyway."

"All right for you," Robin sputtered, almost crying as she pulled *her* ring off and tossed it at Whitney's feet.

Whitney kicked at the snow where the silver band had disappeared. Robin got down on her hands and knees on the doorsill and hunted around in the snow on the porch. When she finally found the ring, she looked up expectantly at Whitney.

"The other one's right here." Whitney pointed at the snow with her boot toe. "You can keep them both. I'm sure you'll find another sucker to give your ring to."

"Whitney!" Robin hurled the ring at her.

Whitney raced up the stairs and kicked snow in Robin's face. Robin smashed Whitney on the back of the head with a snowball. Cold liquid trickled down Whitney's neck as she scooped up another mound of snow. Robin was standing now in the open doorway, gazing at her. Snow had whitened her hair and dark lashes. Tears streamed down Robin's cheeks, and her mouth hung open but no sound came out. Whitney felt her own sobs coming up. She dropped the snow, turned, and ran. Behind her the door slammed.

Whitney cried into the heavy white silence until she was breathless, her misery growing as she approached home. In the garage she tried to compose herself, but her mind wouldn't let her forget the fight so she could stop crying. Why was Robin doing this to her? How could she have been so mistaken about someone? How could she be so blind? She never wanted to see anyone again as long as she lived. She let herself in through the back door and went up to her room. It was the only safe place in the world. She wished she could get a lock for her door.

CHAPTER EIGHT

Fatherly Chats

When her father knocked on the door, Whitney grabbed a book she had already read and opened it. There was a long silence before he finally let himself in. She gritted her teeth, trying to prepare herself for the cross-examination.

"How're you doing?" He stood uneasily just inside the room.

"Okay." Whitney stared into the black print.

"Couldn't you use a little light? It's nearly dark outside."

"I can see fine."

Her father reached above her headboard to switch on the reading lamp. "Mind if I sit down?"

"Where?" Whitney asked.

"Right here on the edge of your bed if there's room."

The phone rang. Whitney strained to hear if her name was being called. Her father cleared his throat.

"Want to put your book away and talk to me for a minute?"

She flung the book aside, stared out the window.

"Your mother's worried about you."

"I didn't do anything."

"I didn't say you did. Has something happened that we don't know about?"

"No."

"You'll feel better if you talk about it." Her father was also staring out the window. "I'm here to help you, Whitney, not to hurt you."

Whitney started to cry.

"Please, let's not have any of that." He pulled his handkerchief out of his pants pocket. "Blow your nose and dry your eyes."

Whitney blew her nose.

"That's better. Now, tell me what's bothering you."

Whitney tried to think of something to say.

"It's better if you talk."

She shook her head.

Her father frowned at her. "I insist you tell me what's going on."

"I'm doing horribly in school." She stole a glimpse at him.

"You've never had trouble before."

Whitney shrugged.

"Does Robin have something to do with this?"

"NO!" she shouted. "I just can't concentrate," she added quickly.

"Well, what can we do to help?"

"Nothing."

"Do you want me to set up a space in the basement so you can study undisturbed? Will that help?"

Whitney nodded.

"You might be feeling bad because of your period, you know. You should be getting it any day now."

Whitney gazed out the window.

"These changes often cause upheavals."

She felt her ears getting hot.

"Well, I'll leave that to your mother. I'm sure she's already explained it to you."

Whitney wanted to die.

Her father patted her head. "Come eat dinner with us like a normal human being. I'll set up a space in the basement for you as soon as I can find the time." Her father stood. "Do you have anything else to say?" he asked as he folded the dirty handkerchief.

Whitney looked puzzled.

"All right, have it your way, but try to make the best of things, pull yourself together. You know how your mother worries."

"Sure, Dad." She tried to smile. "I'll do better."

"That's more like it." He leaned over her, she thought to kiss her, but he hugged her head instead, knocking off her glasses in the process. "You look so much better when you're happy. Smile, Whitney, and the whole

world smiles with you." He fit one of the stems back behind her ear.

The doorbell rang.

He paused in front of her closet mirror to adjust the
knot of his tie. "Wash up now. The Wigginses are here."

A few minutes later Whitney slipped into her place at
the kitchen table. "Did anyone call?" she couldn't help
asking.

Her mother stopped rolling out the biscuit dough and
glanced up at her daughter. "Do you mean Robin?" With
the cutter she pressed circles of dough onto the cookie
sheet.

"Not necessarily."

Mrs. Bennett wiped her hands on her apron. "You two
call each other so much I certainly can't keep track."
She turned to Mrs. Wiggins. "Do you think it's healthy
for a girl Whitney's age to spend all her time with just
one friend?"

"Ma, stop." Whitney rolled her eyes in exasperation.

Mrs. Wiggins glanced from Mrs. Bennett to Whitney,
then back to Mrs. Bennett. "It's not uncommon, I understand, during adolescence, although when my Shirley
was her age I could hardly keep track of all the new
faces."

Mrs. Bennett sighed. "It's hard not to worry."

Mrs. Wiggins jumped from her perch. "Are you sure
I can't do anything?"

"Ma, did Robin call or didn't she? It's important,"
Whitney added, unable now to hide her urgency.

"She might have, dear — I don't remember. But please don't interrupt when we're talking."

Robin, of course, didn't arrive at the usual time to pick her up. Whitney dawdled as long as she dared before hurrying off to school alone; on top of everything else she was going to be late. She slipped into her seat just as the final bell rang. Robin wasn't there. Maybe she was sick. Whitney opened her notebook, hastily diagrammed a sentence. She wasn't prepared for a single class. If she hurried, though, she could at least get the sentences done before first period.

She was trying to figure out which words went with what in the next sentence when Robin sauntered into the room. Whitney watched her slide behind her desk and turn immediately to Susan, the girl behind her. Miss Swan made a mark in her roll book, a check for lateness, but Robin didn't seem to notice or care.

The next bell rang. A page of empty crooked lines lay in front of Whitney: she had gotten only one sentence into position, and sloppily at that. Mr. Polluci hated messes. Getting the lines straight and keeping the words on them was worth more credit than getting the right words on the right lines. Robin did hers in colored pencils and got A's.

But Mr. Polluci seemed to have forgotten all about the homework. He launched immediately into an explanation of a precis. Whitney stared at the back of Robin's head, which tilted first to one side, then to the other as if she were listening, but she had her pad open and was drawing . . . probably Mr. Polluci. He was a wild-looking man with a shock of wavy orange hair and large green-framed glasses, and Robin liked to do caricatures of him, especially when he got all worked up over something. Today, though, he seemed dull and listless. "What about our homework?" Beatrice finally reminded him.

"Ah, yes, I'd almost forgotten. Just pass it up. Will you all just pass up your homework." He ran his hand through his hair, brushing it back off his forehead. "Thank you for reminding me, Miss Walker."

Everyone was giving Beatrice dirty looks except Robin, who was busy with her sketch. Smiling, Beatrice turned off her hearing aid and handed her homework to the person ahead of her. Now Whitney was stuck with all the papers from the kids behind *her*. She got up and was passing Robin when she had an impulse to snatch away her pad and turn it in to Mr. Polluci along with the homework. At the same instant Robin bent over the pad protectively, her nose nearly touching the drawing. Whitney gave the papers to Rodney. As she was passing Robin again, she saw Robin slap both hands over the drawing, then look up at her, very surprised. Whitney sank back behind her desk in despair. It wasn't a carica-ture of Mr. Polluci, it was *she* Robin was ridiculing, and the drawing would circulate . . .

Whitney read the first paragraph of the essay for

which they were supposed to make a precis three times but still didn't get the gist of it. Not only would she get a zero on her homework, she'd get a zero on the class assignment. She stared out the window at the frozen playing field, wishing it were three o'clock and she were home. Once she turned back to the classroom to catch Robin quickly looking away from her and back to her drawing, whatever it was, and Whitney was surer now than ever it was of her. When the bell rang she hadn't written a single word, and Robin was up and gone before she had even gotten her books together.

During geography, although Mr. Palmer kept pausing and looking at her in a funny way, he seemed to avoid calling on her. Whitney felt so relieved that for the rest of the period she laid her head on her desk, her face turned away from Robin. Way off in the distance she heard the bell ring but she couldn't bring herself to move. Suddenly there was a hand on her shoulder. She tried to escape but Mr. Palmer held on. The classroom was empty.

"Wake up." He smiled. "The class is over."

"I'm sorry, I wasn't asleep. I was just — "

"I know." He put his hand up for her to stop. "You're in one of your moods. But don't take it too seriously. It'll pass."

She gathered her books.

"And what's with your friend? Gone like a shot. Not even a hello. You think she's avoiding me because you two have been forgetting to water my plants?"

Whitney clapped her hands over her mouth. She'd forgotten all about the plants.

"Go on, hurry." Mr. Palmer pushed her gently toward
the door. "Go find her. I'm sure she's looking for you
right this minute."

In the corridor Whitney sniffed back her runny nose,
but the tears kept pouring out and her nose kept refilling.

"Wait." Mr. Palmer strode down the hallway after her.
"I'll walk down with you."

Whitney tried to dry her eyes with her fists. He was
walking beside her now. "Here, let me carry your books."
He took the load out of her arms, tucking it under one
of his.

"Was it a bad fight?"

Whitney couldn't help looking up at him. "How did
you know?"

"It's written all over your face." He smiled.

She quickly looked back at the floor. They walked
down the corridor in silence. Mr. Palmer cleared his
throat. "I'll bet you didn't know I was once engaged."

Whitney shook her head. He glanced down at her
again. "You want to know what happened?" Whitney
nodded. "She left me," he continued. "For my best friend,
no less — one month before the wedding."

Whitney couldn't think of what to say.

"And do you know what I did?"

Whitney shook her head.

"I put my fist right through my living-room wall.
Crazy, huh?"

"Did you hurt yourself?"

"Oh, I mangled my hand all right, but that was nothing compared to how I felt inside. We all feel that bad some time or other."

"Yeah," Whitney muttered.

"But then after a while we get over it. My hand healed, so did my heart. Only my pride stayed wounded for a long time afterwards, but even that eventually went away and now look at me, a free man!" He squeezed Whitney's arm. "Have a good lunch." He disappeared through a swinging door into the teachers' lunchroom.

Whitney felt so much better that she started to want the lunch her mother had packed for her, after all. At the end of the lunch line, she was paying the cashier for her milk and ice cream when she heard someone yelling her name. She scanned the room. Jane from her gym class was standing on a chair, waving and motioning her over. Gratefully, Whitney squeezed through the long rows of tables and chairs, avoiding looking in the direction where she and Robin usually ate.

"Robin was looking for you," Jane announced as Whitney emptied her lunch bag.

"Yeah, I'll bet," Whitney mumbled to herself through a bite of her tuna-fish sandwich.

"She said she had something to give you." Jane picked up Whitney's bag of chocolate-chip cookies. "Can I have one?"

Whitney laid down her sandwich and nodded.

Jane ripped open the baggie. "Are you mad at her or

something?" She began munching on a cookie.

"I'm just sick of her, that's all," Whitney said, hoping Robin hadn't told Jane about their fight. But the lie was beginning to make her feel worse than the truth.

"You want to come to my house this afternoon?" Jane helped herself to another cookie. "We could study for the science test together."

Whitney eyed Jane suspiciously. She was trying to decide whether to accept the invitation when out of the corner of her eye she spied Robin and Charlotte crossing the lunchroom, their heads together, laughing at what looked to Whitney like Robin's sketch pad.

"I've got to go." Whitney leapt to her feet.

"So you want to come or not?" Jane finished off the last of the cookies.

"Can't." Whitney was nearly breathless now from the sight of them.

"Why not?"

"I have to go to the dentist." Whitney didn't realize until the words were out of her mouth that she really *did* have to go to the dentist but until that moment had forgotten all about it.

"Aren't you going to eat your ice cream?"

"You can have it."

"Thanks. I'll take your tray back for you," Jane called after her as Whitney pushed her way through the kids in the aisle. Charlotte and Robin had disappeared. Whitney searched both lunchrooms but apparently they had left. Anyway, even if she found them, what would she do? Demand the picture? Threaten to spread some dirt about Robin if she didn't hand it over?

Whitney trudged up the three flights of stairs to the science classroom. Tommy Jensen and Eddie Warfield wheeled around when she opened the classroom door. "You're early," Tommy accused her as she headed for her desk. He had something hidden behind his back. "Did you hear?" He watched her slide into her seat. "Mr. Johnson's sick."

Eddie was opening and closing all the desk lids. "This one," he said to Tommy. He had stopped at Beatrice's desk.

"You'd better not rat on us," Tommy warned Whitney. He dangled the school's opossum by its tail in front of her. The opossum squealed as they stuffed it into the compartment and closed the lid.

Other kids began to wander into the classroom. Whitney watched Beatrice's desk lid move slightly, then fall back into place. Robin made it to the room just as the final bell rang, alone and out of breath. Whitney glared hard at her, but Robin stared at the floor as she zoomed past Whitney.

By the time the substitute teacher arrived, the opossum had escaped from Beatrice's desk and was scurrying up the aisle. Several girls had jumped up onto their seats and begun to scream. Everyone else was running around the room in pursuit of it. The substitute begged them all to return to their desks, but no one paid any attention. Only Robin and Whitney remained in their seats, Robin once again absorbed in her drawing, Whitney too depressed about it to join in the fun. It was Tommy Jensen who finally cornered and captured the frightened animal and delivered it to its cage.

Whitney had a sudden impulse to turn and scribble all over Robin's drawing, but the substitute was watching them very carefully now. Twisting around in her seat to give Robin a dirty look instead, Whitney was surprised to find Robin staring mournfully up at her. Robin quickly looked away. She had taken out her pastels, which she only used on special occasions, and begun filling in the pencil lines.

"No talking, girls!"

Guiltily, Whitney faced forward. For the rest of the period she avoided eye contact with the substitute so she wouldn't be called on.

By the end of the day Robin was all over the place talking and whispering, showing her drawing to just about everyone except Whitney, and it was driving Whitney mad. When the final bell rang, Robin walked to the door with her pad open on top of her books, fussing over her picture. Susan peered over her shoulder at it, then looked back at Whitney. Whitney couldn't stand it anymore. She ran after Robin, caught up with her just outside the classroom door, reached over her shoulder, and snatched away the pad.

Robin whirled. Whitney held the pad behind her back,

but Robin reached behind her and grabbed it. Whitney lunged for it again, this time ripping out three-quarters of the page.

"My drawing, my drawing," Robin cried.

"Here, take your crummy drawing." Whitney caught a glimpse of it as she thrust it at Robin. It didn't look like her at all, but it was her, must be her. She looked up at Robin, who was trying to fit the two pieces together.

"Can I see?" Whitney bent over the pad. "That's not supposed to be me, is it?"

"Maybe."

"But you made me look so nice," Whitney protested.

"So what?"

"I don't look like that."

"Yes, you do," Robin insisted. "Sometimes you do. Here." Robin handed her the torn picture. "You might as well have it."

"For me?" She still couldn't believe her eyes as she stared at the sketch.

"Yeah, but I was gonna surprise you."

Whitney peeked up at Robin. Her lower lip trembled. "I could tape it."

"Right."

Whitney looked down at herself again. "You shouldn't have — "

"Well, I did. Now could we please be friends again?"

CHAPTER NINE

Egypt's Hill

"I see you two are pals again. Just when I was beginning to restore a little peace and quiet to this class." Mr. Palmer rapped the back of Robin's hand with his pointer. He turned to the class. "Now, as I was saying before I was so rudely interrupted." He frowned at Robin. "The iron curtain is not an iron fence as Geoffrey has suggested, but a symbol." He wheeled back around and tapped Whitney's desk. "Of what, Miss Bennett?"

"Of communism."

"Tell me more."

Whitney stared at him blankly.

"Come, come. Communism. What is that?"

"The opposite of democracy."

"A bit circular, Miss Bennett. You all, of course, know what democracy is." No one said anything. "Has anyone read the assignment? Take out a clean sheet of paper."

Notebooks rattled, everyone sighed. "Write definitions of democracy, communism, and the iron curtain."

Whitney wrote the three words, stared at them. Democracy is the opposite of communism, communism the opposite of democracy, the iron curtain the line between the two. She might squeak by. She had read the chapter, but it had all flown out of her head. She didn't seem to be able to retain anything. A couple of kids glanced over at her paper. But what did she know?

"All right. Pass them forward."

Whitney quickly scribbled out her original thought. Mr. Palmer strolled across the room, collecting the test papers from the first person in each aisle. "Open your books to Chapter Twelve and read, all of you. If by some miracle you've already read it, go on to the next chapter. Your final will cover the entire book, whether or not we finish it in class. I have the sneaking suspicion that some of you haven't read a word all spring." He looked hard at Robin.

Whitney opened her book and began reading the chapter again, trying extra hard to concentrate on the meaning of the words. Lunch, three more classes, then she and Robin would race home to change, pick up their dogs, and meet at Jerry's luncheonette for fudgesicles before the dogs yanked them down the hill to Echo Lake. They could wade in the stream — it was warm enough now — and if they could scrape together enough money, rent a rowboat.

The bell rang. Somehow Whitney had gotten through

the chapter again without remembering a word she had read.

"Whitney, hurry." Robin slammed her book. "We'll be the last ones in line again."

Mr. Palmer waylaid them at the head of the aisle. "When are you leaving us?" He handed Robin back her test paper.

"July or August." Robin unfolded her paper. "But it says right here you're not supposed to say anything."

"Leaving?" Whitney accepted her test paper without looking at it. "Who's leaving?"

Robin pointed her finger at her chest. "Me."

"Who says?"

"My father says."

"For how long?" Whitney asked, before she realized this was probably another one of Robin's tricks on Mr. Palmer.

"Forever," Robin answered gaily.

"Oh sure, you wish."

"No, it's true. I just found out last night. I was going to surprise you but *he* ruined it."

Mr. Palmer frowned. "That's what you get for trying to con a good grade out of me. What school system is going to have the honor of Your Highness's presence, may I ask?"

"Very funny. We're moving to Chicago. My dad says we'll be in a suburb that has one of the best school systems in the country."

"A lot of good that'll do you."

"But when are you going?" Whitney still couldn't believe it, and she was beginning to feel angry that Robin was carrying this gag so far.

"As soon as my dad finds a house and we sell this one."

"Well, don't forget your old buddies back east. Some of us will probably miss you, right, Whitney?" Mr. Palmer mussed her hair.

She ducked, still staring amazed at Robin. "Are you really moving?"

Robin nodded. "It's a wonderful opportunity for us all."

"You mean you *want* to go?"

"Why shouldn't I?" Robin looked at her as if she were crazy. "This town is a bore. I'll be glad to get out of here, go someplace new and exciting."

"Yeah." Whitney looked away. If this was Robin's idea of a joke, it wasn't at all funny.

"Don't worry, Whitney." Mr. Palmer put his arm around her shoulder. "We'll do just fine in this boring town without her."

Whitney didn't want his arm there but didn't move.

"Dad says I might be able to get a short-haired terrier" — Robin's voice wavered — "or a miniature poodle of my very own out there."

"You and your dogs." Mr. Palmer slid off his desk. "You two have dogs on the brain. No wonder you can't get anything right on my tests. Now scram before I change my mind and fail you both."

"I thought you said you hated moving?" Whitney

kicked open the classroom door.

Robin caught it. "This is different."

"What's so different about it?"

On the lunch line Robin stared at the back of the head in front of her. "Maybe he won't be able to find a house. Or maybe we won't be able to sell this one. Then we won't have to move." Robin's eyes were watery now, the tears threatening to break from the corners.

Whitney felt confused. "What's the matter?" she asked, feeling sorry for Robin in spite of herself.

"Nothing." Robin wadded up her test paper. "I hate him."

"Who?"

"Who do you think?"

"Mr. Palmer?"

"Oh, you. My father, that's who."

"Why?"

"He's just making that up about the dog. As soon as we get there he'll say he didn't promise, he said maybe, *if* the yard was big enough, *if* Scott didn't have an allergic reaction, if, if, if. And I won't have a dog out there either. He makes me so angry sometimes, I could scream."

"He seems nice to me."

"Do you know what he said to me last night?"

Whitney shook her head.

"That he doesn't like me hanging out in the park all the time, that it's just as well we're moving."

"What's wrong with the park?"

"Don't ask me." Robin tossed the wadded paper across the hallway into the garbage pail.

"Is that why you're moving?"

"I wouldn't be surprised."

"Maybe if you promise to reform, you won't have to go."

Robin shrugged. "He's already flying to Chicago next week." She barely touched her ravioli. Whitney eyed her coconut cake.

"Take it." Robin pushed it across the table.

"You sure?" Whitney took the cake plate, feeling starved all of a sudden.

"Yeah, this stuff stinks. I don't know how I've been able to eat it all this time."

"You want half of my sandwich?"

"Nah, I'm just not hungry." Robin drummed her nails on the vinyl table top. "Wait till Chappy hears. He's still stuck on me, you know."

"I know. You've told me a million times."

"But Geoffrey's so much more appealing. I wish I could get *him* to ask me out." Robin tore the end of a nail off one of her fingers with her teeth. "He probably won't even care when he finds out. School will be out. Everyone'll be on vacation. No one'll even know the difference."

Whitney scraped the last of the icing off the plate. For some reason the cake was making her feel hungrier.

"Boy, does he make me mad." Robin spit out her nail. "Sometimes I think he hates me."

"Are we still going to the park this afternoon?"

"Of course we are," Robin snapped. "Why shouldn't we?"

"I don't know. Now that you're moving . . ."

"Whitney," Robin wailed, "don't be mean."

Whitney opened her mouth to defend herself, but Robin's eyes were filling up again. Whitney stared helplessly at her. "I have an idea." She socked Robin in the arm. "You could live with us."

"Oh, sure." Robin dried her eyes.

"Well, why not?"

Robin wiped her nose on her sleeve and smiled. "Now I could eat a horse."

Whitney gave her the remains of her sandwich.

When they met at Jerry's luncheonette with the dogs, Robin told Whitney that her mother had said her father's promotion wasn't in the bag after all and she wasn't supposed to go blabbing it all over town. At first Whitney felt tricked, then relieved, even if Robin had gotten everybody all excited over nothing. Then she forgave her altogether when Robin treated her to a package of chocolate cream-filled cupcakes.

Halfway to the park Robin stopped. "I'm sick of Echo Lake." She licked cream off her fingers. "Let's go to Egypt's Hill."

"Egypt's Hill?" Whitney was forbidden to go there. "Do you know the way?"

"Sure. My cousin used to go. I got him to explain it to me."

"Explain what?"

"How to get there. What goes on. What's the matter, you chicken?"

"Lead the way." Whitney dragged Lady, who was still straining toward the park, back up the hill. They turned onto a dirt road with a sign at the head of it that said PRIVATE ROAD, NO TRESPASSING.

"Now be quiet," Robin warned. "We don't want to attract any attention. And for God's sake don't let Lady start barking."

At the end of the road they followed a path across a field to a blackberry thicket. Neither one of them had on long pants, and by the time they got through the bushes their legs were scratched and bleeding. "Are you sure this is right?" Whitney examined her scratches.

"There's a clearing ahead," Robin called over her shoulder. They broke out of the woods onto a barren field dotted by three hills, one large one looming directly in front of them, two smaller ones on either side. "That's it." Robin pointed straight ahead. "That's Egypt's Hill."

"What's so great about that?"

"I don't know. Let's climb up and see."

Whitney scrambled up ahead of Robin, who ascended slowly, more cautiously, double-checking all her footholds. Once Whitney was safely on the mossy bed at the top, she peered down over the rocks at her friend and the dogs.

"Holy mackerel." Robin crawled up onto the mossy plateau. "They come all the way up here? I can't believe it." She collapsed, panting, next to Whitney. "Look." She held out her hands. "I'm shaking. That's some scary climb!"

Whitney held out her hands. "It didn't bother me." She stretched out on her back in the sun. "This sure is soft. I wonder how it got so mossy?"

"Someone must've planted it."

Whitney reached above her head and pulled a beer can out from under a bush. "Well, it's true we're not the first ones here." She threw it back into the bushes. Lady pounced on it. Whitney caught her by the tail and pulled her out.

"Whitney?" Robin squatted Indian fashion beside her.

"What?"

"Let's take off our clothes and sun in the raw."

"Nah."

"Come on. No one can see us. There's no excuse now."

"I don't feel like it."

"You never feel like it."

"So what if I don't?"

"You're yellow. I dare you."

"I double-dare you."

"Double-dares go first."

"No, they don't." Whitney sat up. "Dares go first. You're always trying to change the rules."

Robin began unbuttoning her blouse. "Okay for you. Remember, if I do it, you have to." She unzipped her shorts, wriggled them down to her knees. "C'mon." She stood, kicked them off, ripped her blouse off her arms. Still in her socks and sneakers, she straightened, stretched her arms to the sun. "It feels great."

Whitney gazed out over the mile or so of barren field surrounded by woods in order to avoid looking at Robin. Far off she could hear the highway traffic. "But what if we get caught?"

"We won't." Robin turned slowly as if on a pedestal, extending her arms first in one direction, then another. "Look at me, world!" she shouted. "C'mon, Whitney, you'd better not back out now."

Whitney ducked between two bushes, got undressed, and waddled into the open. She sat hunched forward on the moss, her knees tucked under her chin. Dropping to the ground, Robin glanced over at her. "I knew you'd do it. Doesn't the sun feel good?"

"Uh huh." Whitney wrapped her arms around her knees.

Robin stretched out on her back, her hands crossed behind her head. "Relax, will you? No one's going to come."

Whitney leaned back on her palms but still felt uncomfortable. "Let's head home."

"We just got here."

"I'm bored."

"I'll bet you don't even know what they do up here."

"I do so."

"What?"

"Why should I say?"

"To prove you're not lying."

"You're the one who doesn't know." Whitney reached between the bushes for her clothes.

"Wait." Robin sat up. "At least let's sun for a couple of minutes."

"Then we'll go?"

"Definitely."

Whitney flopped to her stomach. Robin rolled to her side, facing Whitney. "Turn over. I want to show you something."

"What?"

"You'll see."

Whitney flipped back over, propped her head and shoulders up with her elbows.

"Lie back," Robin ordered.

Whitney eased down, not taking her eyes off Robin's.

"Are you ready?"

Whitney nodded.

"Don't blink," Robin whispered, as she inched closer. Whitney opened her eyes wide. "Don't blink, I said." Their noses met. Whitney took a deep breath. "Don't blink, don't blink," Robin chanted, as she hugged Whitney's body to her own.

"What're you doing?" Whitney gasped. Suddenly Robin began to tickle her in the ribs. "No fair!" she shrieked.

"I win, I win!" Robin laughed as she rolled away.

Whitney sat up, clutched her stomach, and tried to

quiet the rush of feeling inside her. "What did you do that for?"

Robin sighed, spread-eagled in the sun. "I can't wait to grow up."

Whitney retrieved her clothes.

"Then I can do whatever I feel like doing."

Whitney snapped shut her shirt. "I feel like going home."

"Wait for me." Robin sat up and stuck her sneakers through the legs of her shorts. "What's the matter? You seem mad."

"I'm not." Whitney stuffed her shirttails into her shorts.

"Then why do you look so strange?"

Whitney stooped, picked at a scab on her ankle, and watched the blood ooze out the corner, feeling kind of sick inside. "How come you never gave me my ring back?" she asked finally.

"Whitney!" Robin stamped her foot. "You're the one who threw it away."

Whitney wiped away the trickle of blood with her finger.

"Is that really what's the matter?"

She nodded. At least, she told herself, it was one of the things that had once been the matter.

"If I had known you wanted it, I would've given it to you ages ago."

Whitney stroked Lady's head. "It's not important."

"You're nuts." Robin punched the soft, fat upper part of her arm.

Whitney jerked her arm away.

Robin sprang to her feet. "Last one down's a rotten egg."

Whitney descended slowly. She didn't care anymore about beating Robin.

Robin was waiting at the bottom of the hill. "What's eating you now?" She took Whitney's arm. Together they strode across the field.

At the edge of the woods Whitney stopped. "Robin?"

"Yeah?"

"Don't ever mention to anyone that we've been here."

"No one?"

"No one. This will be our secret place. We'll never bring anyone else here as long as we live. Deal?"

They shook on it, but Whitney still felt uneasy. She lagged behind as Robin led the way through the woods. "We'll write it into our pact, add a clause," Robin called over her shoulder as she stepped up onto the trunk of a fallen tree. "Plus we'll write in an agreement to wear each other's rings from now on, no matter what."

"Even if you move?" Whitney couldn't help asking.

Robin paused on the tree trunk, her arms extended for balance.

But you're not going to move, Whitney started to add, more to reassure herself than as a question, feeling so angry all over again at Robin for threatening to move that she barely noticed the cracking noise as the wood gave way under Robin. Robin's knees buckled; she had fallen to her hands and begun pulling her foot out of the rotten wood when suddenly she screamed. Before Whitney could reach her, Robin had ripped herself free and was crashing through the woods, stumbling and crying as she went.

"What's the matter?" Whitney straddled the log below the cave-in. Something pierced her cheek. She yelped, swatted the air, and jumped to the ground on the other side. She was rising to chase after her friend when something stung her again, this time on the forehead. She screamed: it flew into her mouth. A needle-like stab shot through her tongue. She howled from the pain, flailing her arms at the hundreds of yellow insects swarming around her head. One got her in the eye as she tore through the woods. She cried out again. When she finally escaped them, she could no longer even tell where they had stung her. She collapsed in a heap by the blackberry bushes, her face throbbing from the attack.

Robin gaped at her. "You look awful."

Whitney opened her mouth to say something, but it hurt to move her jaw.

"Quick." Robin grabbed her arm. "Let's go home." Whitney let herself be dragged through the prickers. One eye was swollen shut now, and the inside of her mouth was so sore she could hardly swallow. "Give me

Lady." Robin snapped both dogs onto their chains. "Hurry, Whitney, I'm scared."

"You don't have to walk me home." Whitney went for Lady's leash. "I can manage okay." She slurred her words, barely opening and closing her mouth.

"You sure?" Robin stared at her.

"Positive."

"But why are you swelling like that?" Robin pointed at two red spots on her arm. "I got stung too, but nothing happened to me."

"I don't know." Whitney groaned.

"I'm coming with you." Robin snatched back Lady's leash. Whitney was grateful but didn't say anything. She was beginning to feel worried about what her mother would say.

At the back door Whitney mumbled, "Rememer, we wen' to E'ho La'." Robin nodded.

Whitney's mother took one look at her and gasped, then a low moan set in. They stood just inside the back door on the landing, waiting for her to stop.

"Bees, Mrs. Bennett," Robin finally offered. "We ran right into a hive of them at Echo Lake. It wasn't her fault." She looked at Whitney.

Mrs. Bennett picked up the phone and dialed. "Get in the car, both of you. Dr. Pine, please. Wait, not the dogs too. Leave them here."

After she unleashed the dogs, Robin led Whitney out the door. They sat in the back seat in silence. Mrs. Bennett ran across the yard to the car. "Why do these things always happen to you?" Glancing at Whitney, she groaned again as she backed out the driveway.

"I got stung too." Robin thrust her arm over the seat back.

"Not now, Robin. I'm in a hurry." Whitney's mother drove across town in a way she had never driven before, screaming around corners, stopping suddenly, throwing them both forward against the front seat.

Whitney started to feel scared. "Am I going to live?" She mouthed the words.

"Of course you're going to live, don't be ridiculous."

Whitney looked at Robin, who looked worried too. They ran after Mrs. Bennett up the sidewalk, into the doctor's waiting room, past the nurse and patients, into the examination room.

Dr. Pine came in and studied Whitney. "All right, up on the table, young lady. You all can wait outside." He ushered Robin and Mrs. Bennett out. When he returned he had a needle. He daubed Whitney's arm with cotton. "Now it'll only hurt for a second. You don't want to go around looking like this for the rest of your life." He plunged the needle into her arm. She jumped, started to bawl. "There, there." He patted her on the back. "You're too big to be crying over pinpricks, and anyway you should be used to them by now." He helped her off the table. "Be a good girl and send your mother back in."

Whitney sat across from Robin in the only remaining seat in the waiting room. Everyone stared at her. On her way out, after her mother had returned, she glanced into a small oval mirror hanging on the wall near the door. It nearly scared her out of her wits. One eye, both lips, one cheek, and her chin were swollen to nearly twice their usual size, and there was a large goose egg in the middle of her forehead. Her face didn't even look like a face anymore. She was a freak, a mishap of nature.

CHAPTER TEN

The Stash

One by one Robin flipped over the three cards in the kitty. "Jack, jack, nine. Damn it." She threw her hand on the floor. "Can't we play something else? I hate this game."

"You like it okay when you're winning."

"No, I don't. It's no fun with two. You need three or four."

Whitney gathered up the cards. "How about honey-moon bridge?"

"Same problem."

Whitney shuffled. "Canasta?"

Robin made a face.

"Russian bank?"

"Cards, cards, cards. All we ever do is play cards."

"That's not true. At your house all we do is play board games."

"Well, I'm sick of cards. Think of something else."

Whitney fit the pack in the box. "If it would stop raining, we could play catch."

Robin moaned, writhed on the cold linoleum, and came to a stop on her back, legs spread, arms extended.

Whitney touched her recently swollen face. Although it was completely back to normal, she still felt it often just to make sure. "You look like a dead person," she said to Robin, wondering if it was true that you could die from bee stings or if her mother had just said that to scare her.

"Just one more week, Whitney."

"One week and one day," Whitney corrected her halfheartedly.

She had counted on at least having the summer together but now Robin was moving before school even got out.

"I told you we should've gone to my house. My mother's already finished packing the downstairs. She'll be getting to my room any minute now."

Whitney shrugged. "It's not my fault you're moving."

"If she throws out all my stuff this afternoon, it'll be your fault."

"Robin!" Whitney banged her fist on the couch cushion. "I'll be glad when you move." She regretted having said it when she saw Robin flinch.

Robin sat up slowly. "Well, so will I. I'll make lots of new friends who won't make me play all these boring card games day in and day out."

"I never said you *had* to play."

"Yeah, you just get mad at me if I don't."

"You get mad at me if I don't play your dumb games."

"Well, let's do something different." Robin squatted on the arm of the couch. "How about blind man's bluff?" She did a forward somersault across the cushions.

"Fine," Whitney agreed, hoping it would change Robin's mood. She disappeared into the back room, returned with a handkerchief she'd unpinned from the line. "You go first." She stood over Robin, who lay on her back on the couch staring up at the ceiling. Robin didn't budge, didn't even look at her. "You want to play or what?"

Robin groaned as she sat up. "Go ahead. Tie it on me. The back room's off limits," she called out as Whitney circled the room. "And no cheating!"

Whitney tiptoed in socked feet to the bar, hoisted herself up, reached down under the other side, felt across a shelf until her fingers found a coaster stack. She took one off the top and stood; her head grazed the ceiling.

Robin started towards the bar. Whitney threw the coaster across the room. It hit the wooden arm of the rocker. Robin whirled. It bounced to the floor. Whitney watched it roll to the corner. Robin walked towards the chair, sliding her toes out ahead of her. Then with a sudden turn she walked right into the wall. "Ugh," she grunted, "where are you, Whitney? Give me a hint." Robin faced her again, walking towards her with her arms extended. She found the ledge of the bar. Her hands crept across the counter towards Whitney's feet. Whitney sprang onto the bookcase next to the counter.

"That's not fair, Whitney. I heard you move." Robin felt the corner of the bookcase. Whitney backed against the wall, held her breath, sidestepped on tiptoe to the other end, lowered her foot to the top of the couch back, then brought down her other foot just as Robin's hand groped across the top of the shelf to the wall where her foot had been. "Whitney, you're moving. I know you are." She lunged at the couch, grabbing air.

Whitney flattened her body against the wall. Robin climbed up on the couch and edged across it on her knees, swinging her arm over the seat back as she went. Whitney sucked in her stomach. She felt a little rush of air on her knees as Robin's hand swung by. Robin looked right at her, then at the bookshelf, then at the bar as if she could see. Whitney let out her breath slowly. She was smiling at her success when Robin collapsed, her legs twisting up and back behind her, and whined, "Whitney, where are you, I can't find you." She yanked down the handkerchief just as Whitney leapt off the couch back onto the cushion.

"I'm right here," she grinned, "right behind you all along."

Robin grabbed Whitney's legs, wrapped her arms around her calves. "You cheated, you cheated, I know you did." Her body started to heave.

"What's the matter?"

Robin's back rose and fell, rose and fell with silent

sobs. "I don't know. I just got scared."

"Scared of what?"

"That you'd left me or something, snuck away while I groped around in the dark trying to find you." Robin licked a tear off her upper lip. "You wouldn't do that," she gazed up into Whitney's face, "would you?"

"Do what?"

"I don't know, leave me all alone in the dark."

Whitney shook her head that she wouldn't but didn't understand. She wasn't sure whether Robin was joking.

Robin hugged her knees, then let go, wiping her dripping nose with her finger. "Let's find a new place for our stash."

"What for?"

Robin disappeared into the back room and returned with the plastic container. "Why should you get to keep it?"

Whitney shrugged. "Who wants it anyway?" She ran upstairs, relieved that Robin was her old self again, and stuck her head out the back door. "It's still raining."

Once outside, Robin pointed to the sky. "Look!" Arcs of blue and pink and yellow-green were emerging out of the haze. They gazed at the colors gathering intensity in the vapory sky. "Go get your bike. I'll meet you half-way on Mountain." Robin trotted down the driveway. "And hurry," she called over her shoulder, "or we'll miss it."

Whitney ran back inside. Her mother stopped playing the piano when she got to the living room.

"We're going bike riding. It's not raining," Whitney explained.

"Please be careful, Whitney, the streets are still wet. And take your raincoat in case it starts up again."

"Maaa!"

"Do what I say. I know what I'm talking about." She turned back to the keyboard, picking up where she had left off. *"Gonna take a sentimental journey . . ."* She sang the harmony in deep alto tones. Whitney was struck all of a sudden by her voice, how pretty it was. She wondered why her own was so high and nasal-sounding, and almost couldn't bring herself to break away from the lull of the faraway, unexpressed melody, the deep sad resonance of her mother's voice.

She drifted through the house and went out the back way. She was wheeling down the driveway when she heard her name, clear and hard, with the old familiar edge to it. She braked, glancing over her shoulder. Her mother stood on the front porch with her raincoat. Whitney let her bike crash to the gravel and dragged her feet to the porch. "Thanks," she mumbled. "I almost forgot." She seized the rubber slicker, stuffed it into her bicycle basket.

"And don't be late for dinner!" Her mother's voice was still high and insistent as Whitney zigzagged down Bradford Avenue, waving behind her without looking back. She nearly cracked head-on into Robin's racer as she rounded the bend.

Robin veered around her. "It's too late," she moaned, pointing to the sky.

Whitney looked up. The sun had burned away the rainbow. The wet on the road smoked and steamed around their ankles.

"Now what?"

"Egypt's Hill?"

Whitney felt her face again. "How about Echo Lake?"

"Too public. Anyway, I'm sick to death of that place."

Reluctantly, Whitney followed Robin down Mountain Avenue. Once in the woods they made a wide circle around the fallen log. Whitney got to the top of Egypt's Hill first and immediately started digging up moss. By the time Robin crawled up beside her she had made a hole several inches deep in the earth.

"I brought a pencil to write in the new clauses." Robin panted.

Whitney scooped out handfuls of dirt. "What's the use now?"

"What do you mean?"

"You're leaving. We may never see each other again."

"That's true." Robin chewed on the stubby point. "I guess we don't *have* to write it down." She stuck her arm into the hole. "That's good enough."

Whitney dropped the container in.

Robin peered down at it. "Don't you want to take one last look?"

"No." Whitney threw dirt on top of it. "What for?"

"We might want to keep some of that stuff."

"Like what?"

Robin looked hurt. "You sure are in a hurry to get rid of it."

Whitney tossed in another handful of dirt. "Isn't that what we came here for?"

"Yeah, but . . ." Robin pulled the container back out and brushed the dirt off the plastic top. "I don't know." She loosened the lid.

Whitney reached over, snapped it back on. "Let's just get this over with."

"You're right." Robin scraped a pile of dirt into the hole over the container with her forearm. "That's that." She packed the dirt with her hands.

Whitney gazed out across the field. "Maybe you really *could* live with us."

Robin stomped on the ground. "I can't just leave my parents."

"Why not?"

"Because I love them."

"You do?" Whitney stared open-mouthed at her. "You sure don't talk like you do."

"Everybody loves their parents, dope." Robin seemed to be writing something in the dirt with the toe of her sneaker.

"So maybe I could come with you." Whitney held her breath — she wasn't so sure she loved *her* parents, anyway. "Well, what do you think?"

Robin began rubbing out the lines she had just made. "I think we should get out of here."

"Right." Whitney descended so fast that Robin had to run halfway across the field to catch up.

"Slow down." Robin grabbed her wrist. Whitney pulled her arm free but shortened her strides. "Goodbye," Robin called over her shoulder. "Goodbye, goodbye."

Whitney turned. "Shut up, will you?"

"Why should I? Goodbye, hill. Goodbye, secret place." Robin gestured dramatically behind her. "Don't forget me."

Whitney stalked on. Robin caught up in the woods. "Now what's wrong?" She tugged on Whitney's arm.

Whitney shook her off. "Leave me alone."

"Why?"

"I'm in a bad mood, that's all." She hurried on ahead. Robin trailed behind her, letting a gap grow between them. When Whitney got to the bikes she didn't know whether to wait or not. Well, why should she wait? Robin was nowhere in sight. And now all of a sudden not only did Robin *want* to move, she didn't seem to want Whitney along with her either. Whitney grabbed her handlebars and tried to wrench her bike out from under Robin's. They were stuck, hopelessly tangled. She dropped her bike in order to grab Robin's, shaking it until it came free. Then tipped it over in the other direction, indignantly righted her own bike, wheeled it along the path to the road, secretly wishing as she rode home alone that Robin would suddenly catch up.

Just as the Bennets sat down to dinner, the phone rang. Whitney rushed to the kitchen to answer it. "Hello?" she said hopefully.

"Whitney, do you know where Robin is? I've been delaying dinner nearly an hour."

Whitney swallowed. "Last I saw her she was at Echo Lake."

"You *left* her there?"

Whitney was silent.

"Where exactly did you leave her?"

Whitney took a deep breath. "The woods."

"What woods?"

"Where we leave our bikes."

"Let me speak to your mother."

"MA!" Whitney handed the receiver to her mother, praying she wouldn't get into trouble. When her mother hung up, she stared at the receiver for a moment before turning, hands on her hips. "Whitney?" Her voice was sharp. Whitney tried to look helpful. "Do you know more about this than you're letting on?" Whitney looked puzzled. "Why didn't you girls come home together?"

Whitney shrugged. "She didn't want to leave, I didn't want to be late for dinner."

"You girls should know better than to split up in a place like that. It's not safe."

"What's unsafe about it?"

"If anything's happened to her, I'll feel terrible."

"I could go look for her," Whitney offered, wondering if she would be able to find Egypt's Hill in the dark.

"The Wheelers will be here any minute. You're going with them. Go get a sweater."

"Aw, Ma, do I have to?"

"Whitney Bennett! Of course you have to. Your friend is missing."

Whitney dragged upstairs to her room and yanked a cardigan out of her dresser.

"Be careful," her mother shouted after her as she trudged down the driveway to the Wheelers' station wagon. "And don't go out of their sight."

Whitney didn't dare tell the Wheelers where she and Robin had really been. She led them around the edge of Echo Lake to the Swiss tree, then back to the playground, before she declared that Robin had left the park, she was sure of it now.

"If this is some kind of wild-goose chase . . ." Mr. Wheeler shone the flashlight in Whitney's face.

"Phil." Mrs. Wheeler put her hand on his shoulder. "Calm down." She turned to Whitney. "We're both a bit overwrought, dear. Did you go anyplace *besides* the park?"

"N-no," Whitney mumbled.

"Phil, I'm worried sick now."

"Let's go home. I'll bet she's there right now, eating her dinner in front of the TV while we wander all over the countryside — "

"And if she's not?"

Mr. Wheeler backed out of the parking lot. "We'll call the police. What else can we do?"

Mrs. Wheeler started to sniffle.

"She'll be there, you'll see."

They sped back to Robin's house. Robin's little brother, Scott, sat in front of the TV, an empty plate on the floor by his feet, but there was no Robin.

Mr. Wheeler was on the phone describing his daughter when a car engine died out front.

Whitney ran to the window, Mrs. Wheeler to the front door. "Robin!" She switched on the porch light. "Is that you?"

Robin looked up from the trunk of the car and waved. A policeman had pulled her bicycle out of the compartment and was setting it on the street. Taking hold of the handlebars, she wheeled it up the front walk. The cop honked as he drove off in his patrol car.

Mrs. Wheeler rushed down the steps and grabbed her daughter. "Where have you been?" She cried as she hugged Robin. "We were nearly beside ourselves — "

"Ma, you're hurting me."

"She's back, Phil." With one arm wound around Robin's shoulders, Mrs. Wheeler guided her up the porch steps.

"Hi, Dad." Robin grinned.

"You." Mr. Wheeler gripped her shoulders and shook her so hard her teeth started to chatter. Mrs. Wheeler started to cry. "We've been chasing all over the countryside for you, YOU, YOU — " He sputtered, pushed her away from him, frowned at her. Robin cringed, then he pulled her back and wrapped his long arms around her, his face buried in her hair, squeezing her until she cried out in pain and he thrust her away again. "You've got some explaining to do, girl." He steered her into the house. "Sit there and don't move until I come back." He went to the phone in the hallway.

"Ma, I'm all right." Robin ducked out of her mother's arms. "What're *you* doing here?" She frowned at Whitney.

"We were out looking for you. I took them to the park" — Whitney looked hard at her — "where I *left* you."

"The park?" Robin looked puzzled.

Whitney stared helplessly at her friend.

"Oh, *that* park. I left the park hours ago. Which reminds me, what's the big idea of ditching me?"

Mrs. Wheeler glanced disapprovingly at Whitney.

Whitney felt so relieved she didn't even defend herself.

"When I saw you had given me the slip I decided to ride by myself," Robin continued. "Then I got lost." She winked at Whitney.

Mrs. Wheeler laid her head on Robin's shoulder and started whimpering.

"Ma, I'm okay. But don't let Dad punish me," Robin whispered.

Her mother put an arm around her shoulders again.

Mr. Wheeler stood in the living-room entranceway. "What a humiliation!" He frowned at Robin. "You're gonna have to do a lot of fast talking to get out of this one, young lady. Well? What do you have to say for yourself?"

"I got lost, Dad. Honest." Mrs. Wheeler hugged her protectively. "Please don't look at me like that, Dad. I wasn't paying attention to where I was going, that's all, and all of a sudden I had no idea where I was anymore."

"What? With a mouth like yours you couldn't ask directions?"

"I thought I could find the way back by myself," Robin replied indignantly, "and I did ask eventually. I flagged down a patrol car."

"Don't hurt her, dear. She's home safe and sound. That's what counts."

Mr. Wheeler's hands dropped to his sides.

"Can Whitney stay over?"

"If she calls her mother." Robin's mother looked uncertainly at her husband.

"It makes no difference to me." He shook his finger at Robin. "But one last word of warning. Don't ever let me catch you girls in that park again. It's dangerous business, and no place for two young ladies to hang out the way you do. Understand?"

"But Dad, the park had nothing to do with it."

"Don't argue with me. Do you understand or don't you understand?"

Robin nodded. He embraced her. "But it's not fair, Dad."

He clamped his hand across her mouth. "Not another word out of you. Go up to your room and get ready for bed."

"I'm hungry."

Robin's mother squeezed her again. "I'll bring you a nice tray, dear." She couldn't seem to take her eyes off Robin.

A few minutes later Mrs. Wheeler balanced a tray on each arm in the bedroom doorway. "I'm starting on your room tomorrow, Robin. I want you to throw out everything you can tonight."

"Like what?" Robin took a tray. Whitney followed suit, adding a mumbled "Thanks."

"Take a good look and you'll see." Mrs. Wheeler gestured around the messy room. "Anything and everything you don't need. If you don't do it, I will . . . tomorrow."

"Okay, okay, see you later."

"Don't rush me, young lady, I'm on my way." She opened the door. "And Robin?"

"What?" Robin cut a big hunk of lamb off her chop.

"Don't give us another scare like that. You know how worried your father gets."

"I didn't do it on purpose." Robin stuffed the meat into her mouth. "Anyway, if it were up to him I'd never do anything or go anywhere."

"Don't exaggerate, and don't forget your room tonight. I mean it." She started to ease the door shut.

"Ma?" The door swung back open. "What if I don't want to go?"

"Go where?"

"Chicago."

"Don't be silly, dear. Of course you want to go."

"Well, what if I don't?"

"You'll just have to make up your mind to want to, that's all. Where your father goes, the rest of us go."

"Can Whitney come too?"

Whitney dropped her fork.

Robin picked up her bone and began gnawing on it. Her mother hesitated, clinging to the door edge as if waiting for Robin to say more, but Robin seemed to have lost interest. "Want this?" She passed Whitney a slice of buttered bread. "Well, can she?" Robin still didn't look up. Mrs. Wheeler was staring at Whitney now. Maybe she was trying to decide whether she wanted her around or not. Whitney glanced shyly at her, trying to look as appealing as possible.

"Whitney's parents would be heartbroken if we kidnapped her to Chicago." Mrs. Wheeler laughed nervously. "Isn't that right, Whitney?"

Whitney shook her head vigorously, although she knew she was supposed to agree.

"Now, don't forget, girls, there are seconds, if you like. I'll be cleaning up the kitchen if you need me."

"Don't worry, we won't." Robin's words were muffled by a mouthful of food.

"Don't talk with your mouth full, dear."

"I won't." Robin enunciated the syllables, showing off her masticated food again. "If Whitney stays, I stay."

"Don't be silly."

"Bye, Ma."

"You girls can write to each other. You've always wanted a pen pal."

"BYE, MA," Robin shouted.

Mrs. Wheeler slammed the door. Robin looked up from her plate. She seemed to be listening to her mother's footsteps receding down the hallway. "Maybe we could stow you away in the moving van."

Whitney ripped a long strip of meat off her chop.

"But don't you want to know where I went?"

Chewing the piece of juicy meat slowly, Whitney imagined herself rolled up in the living-room carpet, speeding across the country to Chicago.

"Can I have your bone when you're finished?"

Whitney nodded as she tore out the tenderloin. "This is yummy."

"I really didn't go anywhere." Robin watched Whitney suck on her chop. "And I really got lost."

Maybe Whitney could squeeze into Robin's trunk. She left a big chunk of fat on the tail of the bone for Robin.

"Gee, thanks." Robin accepted the bone gratefully. "But I'll tell you a secret, if you promise not to rat on me."

Whitney nodded, folded the bread, took a bite. Her parents would be glad to be rid of her.

Robin sucked the marrow out of the back of Whitney's bone. "I did it on purpose."

"Mmmm." Whitney used the rest of her bread to sop meat grease off her plate.

Robin dropped the second bone on her plate. "Want to know another secret?"

Whitney nodded.

"I went back."

"I thought so."

"But I got tired after a while, just sitting up there. I had to do something to pass the time."

"Yeah." Whitney licked her fingers.

"Were they terribly worried?"

"Not really."

Robin looked disappointed.

"Is that why you did it?"

"Of course not!" Robin looked away. "And now on top of it all I'm supposed to throw away half my stuff, just so there'll be less to carry." She surveyed the room. "Nothing's working anymore."

"What do you mean?"

"I mean I'm sick of all this waiting around. I wish we'd move tomorrow and get it over with." Robin flopped on her bed. "I'm not sorting through anything. Let her throw it all out. I don't care anymore *what* she does with it."

There was a long silence. "Did you dig it back up?"

Robin raised her head to stare at Whitney. "Yeah, how did you know?"

Whitney shrugged.

"Are you mad at me?"

Whitney shook her head.

"I wanted to reread everything." She looked at Whitney for signs of disapproval. Whitney scraped her plate onto Robin's and stacked them. "Just for the fun of it, you know?" Whitney didn't say anything. "You could too, if you wanted to." Whitney nodded. "I'll bet you do when I'm gone."

"Gone?" she started to say, but said instead, "What do I need to look at that stuff for? It's fine with me if I never see it again."

"Yeah." Robin closed her eyes. "I know how you feel."

Whitney picked up the dishes. Robin opened one eye. "Leave those. She'll get them."

"But — "

"If you want to do something, you can help me sort through this mess."

CHAPTER ELEVEN

Mothers and Daughters

Robin gave the proprietor a dollar and lowered her foot into a new aluminum boat on the far side of the dock.

"Hey, girlie, that one ain't in use. Over here." He gestured to a run-down, beat-up boat with heavy wooden oars bolted into oarlocks.

"We want this one." Robin dropped to the seat.

"I said that ain't in use." He strutted across the dock, extended a thick, hairy hand. "Come on out."

Robin looked up at him, then at Whitney watching from the end of the dock.

"Don't give me no trouble."

Robin used his hand to hoist herself back up to the platform. "Then give us aluminum oars. The others are too heavy." Robin was bent over slightly, one arm folded across her stomach. The proprietor untied the wooden boat and threw two cushion life preservers into it.

"I don't *want* that one."

He pulled the boat around the end of the dock. "Sorry, this is all I got available."

Robin eyed all the newer lightweight boats roped together on the far side of the dock. "Then give me back my dollar."

"You already used up more than a dollar's worth of my time. Now hop in and stop making a nuisance outta yourself."

"You give me back my money or I'll report you."

The old man chuckled and swung the boat back to its mooring. "Who you gonna report me to?"

Robin was doubled over now. "My father."

"Hunh," he grunted as he looped the rope around the post.

"I'll row if the oars are too heavy for you," Whitney offered.

"That's not the point," Robin said pointedly, wrapping both arms around her stomach. "I'm reporting you to my father," she snapped at the boatman. "You wait and see if you don't hear about this," she added before she stalked off the dock, still bent over.

Whitney caught up with her at the concession stand. "How can you tell your father? You're not even allowed to be here."

"Don't you think I know that? I had to tell him something, moron. I couldn't let him do that to us."

"Well, don't blame it on me."

"I'm not blaming it on you, but how come I always have to do all the talking?"

"You don't have to. No one asked you to."

"Well, I'm sick and tired of sticking up for you."

Whitney gazed out at the lake, her back to Robin.

"I'm sorry." Robin leaned against the brick wall of the stand. "I just don't feel good, that's all."

"You got a stomachache?"

"Not exactly. I don't know what it is. I think I have to go to the bathroom." Robin disappeared around the corner to the ladies' room behind the stand.

Whitney turned, leaned on the counter, and stared longingly at the tiered shelves of candy. The boy behind the counter speared a hot dog on the rotisserie. Whitney dug into her shorts pocket: three cents and some stuck-together Green Stamps from Mrs. Wheeler that she had forgotten to give to her mother. The boy turned, started to take a bite, then stopped. "You want somethin' or what?"

Whitney fingered the change in her pocket. "You got any two-cent mints?"

"Just what you see in front of you." Half the hot dog disappeared into his mouth.

"How much is that nut roll?"

"Twenty cents, girlie. Everything's twenty cents 'cept the double bars. They're twenty-five. Ice cream's thirty."

Whitney nodded. "I'll be right back." She hurried into

the ladies' room, spied Robin's shoes in the last stall. "Robin?" she whispered. "You all right?"

"Come in here." Robin sat doubled up on the toilet. "Quick. Somebody'll see us."

Whitney squeezed into the stall. "What's the matter?"

"I'm not sure, but I think it's my period." Robin grabbed Whitney's arm. "What should I do?" She looked up expectantly.

"Wait until it stops?"

"What if it doesn't?"

Whitney shrugged. "We can't stay in *here* all afternoon."

"Come home with me, Whitney."

"What for?"

"It might be something awful. Besides, I don't feel so hot." Robin wrapped her arms around her middle and groaned.

"Sure, I'll come, but let's get out of here."

"Maybe I should get one of those things out of the machine?"

"Yeah," Whitney agreed, not at all sure what they should do.

"You have a quarter?"

Whitney dug out her change. "Just pennies."

Robin handed her a dollar. "Get change at the stand."

"Right." Whitney left the stall, then turned the knob of the machine. The machine clicked but nothing came. She didn't want to face that boy again but forced her feet back outside and around the corner to the front of the stand. This time he was leaning on the counter, sipping a soda.

He put down his paper cup when he saw her. "What do *you* want?"

"Change," Whitney said in a meek voice.

"No change here, sister."

"Give me that nut roll, then." He took her dollar, tossed the candy bar on the counter in front of her, and slapped down some change. Whitney scooped it off the counter without counting it and ran. "I had to buy something," she explained to Robin as she pushed through the heavy rest room door. Robin didn't answer. "Robin? Robin!" she screamed.

"Shut up, I'm right here. What took you so long?"

"I told you, I had to buy something. He wouldn't give me change."

"What'd you get?"

"A nut roll."

"Ugh." Robin groaned. "You know I don't like those things."

"What's wrong with them?"

"They stick to your teeth."

Whitney inserted a quarter and turned the knob of the machine. A cardboard container plopped onto the tray below. Seizing it, she banged on the stall door.

"Hand it under."

She reached down below the door.

"Where's the nut roll?"

"Right here."

"Save me half."

"I thought you didn't like them." Whitney started for the door.

"Don't leave me," Robin whined.

"I'll be outside. It stinks in here." Whitney's mouth started to water for the salty caramel, but she waited until Robin emerged, walking stiffly. "You all right?" Whitney unwrapped the candy bar.

"I don't think so. Give me some."

Whitney eyed the fat log of nuts, visually finding the middle. Then she pressed her thumbnails together to bend it in half. A long string of caramel hung between the two halves. She pulled them apart; the extra goo went with the left half, which she gave to Robin.

Robin stuffed it into her mouth. "I feel starved all of a sudden." She pushed the candy back into her cheek. "My stomach hurts and is hungry all at the same time."

"Are you still bleeding?"

"I'm not sure." She made a face as she chewed.

Whitney liked the way the caramel stuck first to her back uppers, then her back lowers. It spread the sweet taste all over her mouth and stayed there a long time after the candy was gone.

"I could eat a whole pot of spaghetti." Robin held her growling stomach. "Where's my change?"

Whitney dug the change out of her pocket.

"Be right back." Robin walked bowlegged to the front of the concession stand. When she returned, she was licking chocolate off the corners of her mouth.

"Here." She handed Whitney another nut roll.

"Let's go home." Whitney said. Robin followed Whitney across the park. "I'm so uncomfortable, it's driving me crazy."

Whitney slowed down to take her arm. "I'll help you, if you'll walk right."

"Do you think everyone knows?"

"Probably."

"Do you think my mother'll be mad?"

"Mine would be. Can you ride your bike?"

"I don't think you're supposed to."

Whitney righted Robin's bike for her.

"Don't get too far ahead of me." Robin fit herself gingerly on the seat. Whitney zigzagged back and forth across the road behind Robin as she pedaled slowly up the hill. Just short of the crest, Robin stopped. "Whitney, I feel awful." She started to breathe oddly, as if she were going to cry.

"Not here." Whitney remounted her seat. "Concentrate on getting home. You'll feel lots better when you get home."

"Wait for me." Robin pedaled hard to catch up.

Robin's mother was sitting on a carton in the middle of the living room, staring vacantly out the back window. Robin stopped short in the living-room entranceway. "Mom?"

Her mother lifted her chin from her hands and looked at Robin almost as if she had never seen her before. "Yes, dear?" She seemed to be studying a stack of boxes in the corner now, piled nearly as high as Whitney. Whitney felt uneasy. Everyone was acting so strange. She started counting the cartons scattered around the rest of the room.

"I'm bleeding, Mom."

"Bleeding?" Her mother looked up again. "Wash it thoroughly and put on Mercurochrome. You'll have to dig it out of the box just outside the upstairs bathroom."

Robin started up the stairs. Whitney followed. "But you don't understand, Mom."

"Yes, dear," Mrs. Wheeler murmured. "The Band-Aids are in that box too, if you need one. It says BATHROOM on the side."

Robin climbed a few more steps before she stopped again. "But I can't put a Band-Aid on it, Ma, it's all over my pants."

Whitney was surprised to hear Mrs. Wheeler moan the way her own mother moaned. She was at the bottom of the stairwell now, peering up at them. "Don't tell me you've got your period?"

"I don't know."

"Not now." She used the banister to pull her weight up the stairs. "Of all the times to pick for *this* to happen." She passed Whitney without even a smile or nod or hello, her eyes on Robin. "Come." She patted her behind. "Let's have a look."

Whitney sat on the top step on the hard floor (the carpet had been removed) while they disappeared into the bathroom. The upstairs corridor was also lined with boxes, piled against both walls.

When they reappeared, Robin was walking right and smiling. "Can Whitney stay for dinner?" she asked.

Mrs. Wheeler set a box on Robin's dresser and paused in front of the dresser mirror to stare at her reflection. "No, dear, not tonight." She brushed a wisp of hair off her forehead.

"Why not?" Robin asked testily.

"Because I said not. I want you to help me pack the china tonight."

"Aw, Ma — "

"No arguments."

"Whitney can help too." Robin turned. "Right, Whitney?" Whitney looked at Mrs. Wheeler but didn't say anything; she had never been turned down before. Why wasn't she wanted now, when she had been so helpful? She nodded mutely.

"I said no and that's final. And in the future, dear, don't invite a guest to dinner in front of the guest. It's impolite."

Robin flung herself on the bed and faced the wall. Whitney got up to leave. A guest. She was considered a guest. She had always thought she was practically a member of the family. "See you tomorrow," she said from the door. Robin didn't respond, didn't even look up.

Whitney hesitated at the head of the staircase, glancing back into the room at Robin's mother, who was still gazing at herself in the mirror. "I hate you." She heard Robin's voice assert the words out loud to her mother — something Whitney had never dared say to her own mother, although she had felt it often enough. Robin's door slammed and Whitney heard a crash (Robin had thrown something?), then silence, everywhere silence, as if the house had already been evacuated.

Whitney hung around in the kitchen of her family's house, not knowing what to do with herself. Finally, she said casually to her mother, who was tending the pots on the stove, "Robin got her period."

"Take the dog out, Whitney." Her mother lowered a flame. "You've been neglecting her lately."

Lady sat at Whitney's feet. "Why me?"

"Do you remember, my dear, way back when we discussed whether we were going to get a dog, that this was never going to be a problem?"

"Please, Ma —"

"Go on, she hasn't been out since morning."

"Why haven't I gotten my period?"

"Some girls get it sooner than others. What's the rush?"

"How come you never told me about it?" Whitney asked the question without thinking, but now her mother was looking at her so oddly that she regretted it.

"Why, you know very well, Whitney Gabriel" — her mother paused, seemed to be formulating the rest of her response — "I got a book for you ages ago explaining all about those things. We even looked at some of the pictures together."

"We did?"

"We most certainly did." Her mother sounded insulted. "At least I tried. You didn't want to be shown, as I recall. You informed me in your usual stubborn fashion that you weren't a first-grader anymore and could read by yourself."

Whitney did remember vaguely now some pictures that had repulsed her, but had she even bothered to read the book? What she mostly remembered was being the one who had to return the book to the library.

"Poor girl," Whitney heard her mother murmur to herself as Whitney let Lady out the back door.

Who was a poor girl? "Poor me," Whitney chanted to herself as she chased Lady around the barbecue pit. "Poor Robin." She heaved a rubber ball across the yard. Lady retrieved it to the stump where she sat. "Poor Robin." She heaved the wet slobbery ball again. That made more sense. She examined old scrapes on her legs, ripped a scab off her knee. The blood came up slowly. She dabbed it. The sight of her own blood fascinated her. The thought of bleeding the way Robin was, though, frightened her. "Please, God," she prayed, "don't let it happen to me."

"Phone," her mother called from the door. Whitney leapt off the stump. "Where's the dog?"

Whitney gazed around the yard. "Gee, I don't know."

"If the dogcatcher gets her, Whitney, you're paying the fine."

"Lady!" she shouted. "Lady, Lady!" She picked up the ball lying in the grass near the stump. Lady reappeared through the back hedge, bounding toward Whitney and the ball she held out as bait. When Lady lunged for it, Whitney grabbed her chain and dragged her back indoors. "I'll take it in the basement." She ran downstairs.

"Hi, Robin," she said.

"How did you know it was me?"

Whitney shrugged.

"I just had a terrible fight with my mother," Robin whispered.

"I know. Why?"

"I think she's mad at me 'cause I got my period. She says I couldn't have gotten it at a more inconvenient time."

"Do you get to stay home from school?"

"That's hogwash, she says, you're just supposed to act like everything's normal."

"Why?"

"I guess so people won't know you've got it."

"Are you still leaving on Saturday?"

"I guess so."

"Will you be too sick to spend the night here tomorrow?"

"I don't think so. I can't ask now, though, 'cause she's too mad."

"If you spend the night here, at least you'll be out of their way."

"Yeah. Here she comes, I'll call you later." The line went dead.

The phone was still glued to Whitney's ear when her mother bent over the banister to ask her to set the table. She banged the phone down in its cradle.

"Now why did you do that?" Her mother sounded hurt.

"No reason."

"I've told you a thousand times, Whitney, not to put your filthy shoes on the furniture where other people sit." Whitney pulled her legs out from under her, planting her sneakers on the floor. "Are you coming?"

"Why do I always have to set the table?"

"Because you happen to be here. Anyway, you don't *always* set the table. If anyone *always* sets the table, it's me. Now come give me a hand, just for the novelty of it."

Whitney hated setting the table, would rather do just about anything else. She followed her mother to the kitchen and yanked the silverware drawer out. It crashed to the floor. Her mother moaned. "I'm sorry." Whitney was down on her hands and knees instantly, righting the tray, collecting scattered forks and knives. "I didn't mean to do it."

"DON'T PUT THEM BACK WITH THE CLEAN!" her mother's voice screamed. "They all have to be washed now. Oh,

146

God, give me those." She snatched the knives and forks out of Whitney's hand; she was crying now.

Whitney started to cry too, she didn't know why. "I'll do it," she whimpered from the floor. "I'll wash them all."

"Just get out of my way. That's the biggest favor you could do me right now."

Whitney paused in the kitchen doorway. "Can Robin spend the night tomorrow night?" She knew it was the wrong time but couldn't help asking.

"NO!" Her mother plugged up the sink.

"Why not?" she persisted.

"Because it's my birthday tomorrow night. Your father's taking us all out to Snuffy's for dinner."

"Can Robin come too?"

"No, I said No!"

"She could pay for herself."

"It's my birthday, Whitney Gabriel, not that that makes any difference to you."

It was true, Whitney had forgotten all about her mother's birthday. She hadn't even put aside any of her allowance to buy a present. Why hadn't her father said anything? Maybe he had forgotten too? Robin's last night and she had to go out to dinner with her parents? She hung around while her mother set the table, following her broad back from place setting to place setting, waiting without thinking for the hard, determined expression on her mother's face to soften. "What would you like for your birthday?" she finally asked timidly.

Her mother turned to stare at her daughter. The hardness was gone but now she looked sad. "Please don't bother." She glanced out the window at their car pulling into the driveway. "I don't want you spending your money on me." She had on an apron, one that Whitney had never seen before. Whitney was struck by how pretty she looked. She had an impulse to throw her arms around her mother's neck and beg her please not to feel bad but she didn't move.

Her father dropped his briefcase by his armchair in the living room and loosened his tie. "What have we here?" He paused in front of them, glancing from one to the other. "A secret, huh?" He mussed Whitney's hair, leaned down to kiss her mother. Her mother turned her face away. The kiss grazed her cheek. "How much time before dinner?"

"Half an hour."

He yanked off his tie and unbuttoned his collar. "Make it an hour."

"An hour? The roast will dry up. Everything will — "

"Take the roast out. I need to unwind."

The hard expression had returned. It was set now against Whitney's father.

"You can do that, can't you?"

"I guess so," Mrs. Bennett muttered.

"Good. Wake me in an hour."

Whitney felt sorry for her mother. She followed her back to the kitchen and watched her take out the roast, cover it with foil, and turn off all the burners. "Want to play gin rummy?" Whitney asked. Maybe she could get her mother's mind off her troubles.

"Not now."

"After dinner?" Whitney pressed.

"We'll see," her mother mumbled. She turned on the exhaust fan, seemed to be watching the smoke funnel up into the aluminum. Then she untied the apron and hung it on a peg next to the stove. "Don't you have homework to do?" She glanced uneasily at Whitney, who was still staring at her.

"Nope."

"Well, then." She paused. "Why don't you cut some roses for the dinner table?"

Whitney nodded. Her mother opened a drawer. "Use these shears." She handed the scissors to Whitney. "And the green vase under the sink."

When Whitney returned with the roses, her mother was gone. It took three vases to hold them all. She set one on the dining-room table, one on the buffet, one on the living-room mantle. Then she surveyed her work — had she picked too many? She took the most open rose — a white one — and broke off the stem, floating the flower in a crystal candy dish which she set next to her mother's plate.

It wasn't until they all sat down to eat that her mother noticed the flower.

"Happy birthday a day early," Whitney said shyly.

"That's sweet of you, dear." Mrs. Bennett served vegetables onto a plate of meat her husband had handed down before giving it back to Whitney. "I hope you left a few blooms on the bushes." She laughed nervously.

Whitney frowned. "There's plenty more left for you tomorrow on your *real* birthday."

"No more. Please."

They ate in silence.

Mysteriously, during the clean-up the floating white rose disappeared. Later, after everyone had left the kitchen, Whitney dug the blossom out of the garbage and started to rinse off the coffee grinds, but then instead she dropped it into the sink disposal. She threw the switch and listened to it churn, shuddering as she imagined her hand being mangled and digested into the bowels of the house.

CHAPTER TWELVE

The Parting

In homeroom at the end of the day Miss Swan treated the class to cookies and soda while one by one they told what they had liked most about their first year of junior high school. Most kids mentioned a teacher they liked (no one said Miss Swan) or a subject (the majority said gym) until Elwood said it had been stimulating having a different teacher for every subject. Miss Swan gave him a smile of approval. "I'm glad to hear at least one of you is interested in learning. After all, that's what education is all about."

"Next," someone yelled, a spokesman for the general impatience of the entire class. It was three thirty and they were all still confined to their seats. Susan finally said she liked Miss Swan's sewing class best. More groans, and a flush of pleasure on Miss Swan's pasty face.

"Robin?" Miss Swan hurried on.

"What I liked best about this year," Robin drawled, surveying the room, all the bored faces turned to her, "was Whitney."

There was a silence, then someone giggled, infecting the others. "Oh, brother," Chappy said from the back of the room.

"Well, Robin." Miss Swan seemed nervous now. "That doesn't exactly have to do with school, does it?"

"School?" Robin looked dismayed. "School was all right." The whole class burst out laughing.

"Ssh." Miss Swan put her finger to her lips. "Please, class, let's let the others have a chance."

Everyone shuffled and sighed during the turns of the people in the last row. Then they were finished, waiting on the edges of their seats to be dismissed. Miss Swan cleared her throat. "As you all know, Robin won't be back after today. Let's wish her well by singing 'For She's a Jolly Good Lassie.'" She began the first stanza in a low, throaty voice. Some kids drifted up an octave. Others didn't make it. Whitney clapped her hands over her ears.

Robin didn't seem to mind, though; she grinned throughout the song, and when it was over popped out of her seat and said, "Thank you one and all. Three-oh-one is the best homeroom in the school." Everyone clapped and cheered. She held up her hand. There was silence. "And now . . ." All eyes went back to her. "I'd just like to say . . ." She paused. "Class dismissed!"

Everyone leapt from their seats, laughing and hooting.

"Throw your cups and napkins away on your way out," Miss Swan pleaded, holding up the garbage pail.

Whitney waited while Robin emptied her locker onto the corridor floor, feeling awkward and shy. She finally whispered, "How's your period?" not knowing what else to say.

"It's nothing. It doesn't even hurt. Charlotte's crazy."

"Yeah, she'll do anything to lie around all day." Whitney bit her lip. "Say, thanks for saying that in front of the whole class."

"Ah, it was nothing." Robin looked embarrassed, her focus shifting suddenly from the mess on the floor to Chappy, who was approaching them from behind.

"Can I carry some of that stuff for you?" He squeezed in between them.

"Sure." Robin heaved a pile of papers into his arms. "You gonna walk us home?"

"Maybe. You two seem pretty stuck on each other. I don't know if a man is exactly welcome around here."

"Men are welcome, boys are not," Robin chanted in a singsong voice.

Chappy and Whitney hurried down the corridor after her. "Well, in that case," he said, grinning, "you want to go to the luncheonette for one last hot fudge sundae?" He held the door open.

Whitney's heart sank. Robin glanced uneasily at Whitney. "If Whitney can come too."

Chappy squinted at her, shrugging helplessly. "I guess so. But I don't have enough money to treat you both."

"No. Thanks anyway." Whitney rushed ahead of them to the corner.

"Hey, Whitney, wait. Let's at least walk through town together."

Whitney had planned to ask Robin to help her pick out a present for her mother, but now she would have to do it alone. She ducked into a drugstore. When she came out again Robin and Chappy were far down the street. She followed them for a while at a distance before stopping in the middle of the block in front of the five-and-dime. They disappeared into the luncheonette. She imagined finding them in a booth, their heads together across the table (or maybe they would be sitting side by side?), giggling and whispering. She drifted into the revolving door of the five-and-dime. The door pushed her around and emptied her out inside the store next to the electric rocking horse and picture booth. What did they talk about, anyway? Would Robin tell Chappy about her period? Would Whitney be included in the story?

She roamed up and down the aisles: stationery, school supplies, cosmetics, clothes. She had $4.75, which her father had advanced to her. Hardware, plants, birds, fish, toys. She walked on. Candy. She stopped. Chocolate snowdrops, goober peas — a whole bin of them — light and dark caramels. If she had any money left over, she would get a quarter-pound bag of the goobers and a quarter-pound bag of caramels. Jewelry, kitchenware, sewing items. She was really too old to buy her mother presents in the five-and-dime, but she didn't have enough money to go anywhere else. Everything looked so junky, and she hadn't the faintest idea what her mother needed. A fancy pincushion? A crystal butter dish? A flowered scarf? She rejected them all, studied the jewelry again. A gold rose pin with a long stem and two gold leaves caught her eye. It cost $3.25. "Is it real?" she asked the girl behind the counter.

"Whadaya mean, real?" The girl leaned on the register.

"Is it real gold?"

The girl nodded. "Real enough. You want it?"

"Could you put it in a box for me?"

"No boxes." The girl yawned. "So, you want it or not?"

"I — I'm not sure." Whitney tried to think whether her mother even wore pins. She wore earrings sometimes, Whitney was sure of that, but pins? It occurred to her that she barely noticed anything at all about her mother. At this very instant she couldn't even bring her mother's face to mind, much less whether she wore pins. She glanced at her own reflection in a mirror on the glass counter. She looked like her mother, people said. But Robin said that wasn't true; she didn't look like anybody except herself. Whitney liked that idea — except when faced with the reality of herself in the mirror; she had the oddest-looking face she'd ever seen. She hastily bought the pin and hurried home.

Whitney had folded a piece of yellow construction paper back and forth into three sections to make a card to go along with the gift and was racking her brain for something to write when the phone rang. Her mother and father were dressing, so she had to race down to the kitchen extension. Robin was spending the night at Charlotte's, of all places — her whole family was, because all the linens were packed. Did Whitney want to come over in the morning and watch the movers load the van, with her and Charlotte? Her and *Charlotte*!

Whitney swallowed. "Sure, why not?" She tried to hide her disappointment. "What time?"

"The movers are coming at eight. As early as you can. Maybe they'll let us help. Anyway, it'll be fun to watch."

"Yeah," Whitney grumbled, "some fun."

"What's the matter with it?" Robin asked defensively.

"Nothing. Nothing at all."

"I'll see you in the morning, then." Robin hung up.

Whitney went back to her room. Robin and Charlotte? She and Robin weren't even going to spend their last time together alone? Didn't Robin care?

Whitney stared at the blank sheet of construction paper. She had always been so good in the past at thinking these things up; why couldn't she now? She drew and colored three balloons on the front fold, then brought their strings down to a hand which she erased and drew again. It still looked like a six-year-old's drawing. Robin could do this stuff with her eyes shut. Whitney crumpled the paper.

Actually, she thought, after three balloons were successfully scattered across a new blue piece of paper, she should fill the sky with them, one for each year. But how old was her mother? She remembered vaguely that her mother had been twenty-eight not too many birthdays back. Twenty-nine, thirty, thirty-one, thirty-two? She couldn't be sure. *Fly high,* she penciled in elephant letters at the bottom of the card; *on your birthday,* she wrote inside, drawing underneath a cartoon devil that was supposed to be her; then, on the last flap, *Your loving daughter,* a cartoon angel looking down at the devil, *Whitney* in flowery script. On the back she printed *Heartfelt Card Co., Inc., 50 cents.* She examined her work, wishing more than ever that she could draw like Robin could. This would have to do. She made an envelope, inserted the card, slipped the pin inside, pasted the flap shut. It was the work of a child, not an adult! She threw the bulky envelope across the room. It landed on the windowsill.

"Whitney!"

"What?"

Her mother opened the door and peeked in. "You're not even dressed."

"It'll only take a second."

"What've you been doing all this time?" Whitney opened her mouth to protest but her mother went on. "Well, hurry up. You know your father doesn't like to be kept waiting."

Whitney and her mother piled into the car, leaving her father behind to lock up. Then they waited in silence for nearly five minutes before he joined them. Whitney stopped sucking on a sourball to ask if she could order what she wanted for dinner.

"Anything within reason," her father replied.

"A hot dog and French fries."

He sighed. "It's a waste of my hard-earned money to take you out to dinner."

Then why are you taking me? Whitney wanted to ask. Why can't I stay home and have a TV dinner? Robin was probably at Charlotte's now, watching TV.

At the dinner table Whitney decided she wanted a T-bone steak, and when her father ordered her a child's platter of ground sirloin, which he insisted was basically the same thing, she burst into tears. "I'm not a child," she blurted out, wiping her nose on her sleeve. "I'M NOT!"

"Ben." Her mother put a hand on her father's. "Let her have what she wants, just this once."

"But Marge, she'll never eat all of that, for God's sake. She —"

"Please, Ben." She squeezed his hand. "For me. On my birthday."

He frowned at Whitney, pulling out his handkerchief. "Blow your nose." Whitney took the cloth. "And stop crying."

She blew her nose. Her father flagged down the waiter to change the order. She stopped crying but continued to sulk. She didn't feel hungry at all now, didn't want the damn steak. When the salads came, Whitney got one too. That perked her up. She ate the whole thing in spite of her father's disapproving glances. Her parents sipped their drinks while waiting for the main course, neither one of them touching his or her salad. Whitney helped herself to a breadstick. Her father took the basket away, set it between her mother and himself, and warned Whitney to save room for her steak, which he personally was going to make sure she ate every bit of.

Whitney had no trouble at all finishing her steak, and the bone went into a doggy bag for Lady. During the birthday-package opening her mother didn't even try on the pin. "It's a lovely card," she said instead, rereading it as if it were the real present. Whitney was disappointed. She had hoped her mother would like the gold rose.

Whitney finished her hot fudge sundae but still felt hungry; she felt this empty space, as if there were a hole inside her. Soon maybe they would move too. It was about that time — the house was completely repainted and decorated, except the basement. They'd turn that into a rec room, then they'd move, maybe to Florida where they had almost moved last time. A house right on the beach. Whitney would go swimming every single day of the year. Boy, would Robin ever be jealous of her then! Where Robin was going she couldn't swim in an ocean at all, not even on summer vacation.

❖

Back home, Whitney watched Lady gnaw happily on her bone on newspaper in the kitchen corner, then after a while she wandered to the refrigerator and opened it. How could she possibly be hungry? Her mother would say, your father's right. You don't know when to stop. Whitney knew you stop when you've had enough, but right now she felt as though she could never get enough. She shut the refrigerator and started to dial Robin, but then she remembered Robin was at Charlotte's and she hung up.

"Coming to bed, dear?" her mother called from the kitchen doorway.

"Are we going to move again?"

"Why do you ask that?"

Whitney shrugged. "Just curious."

"Have you said your goodbyes to Robin?"

"She's not gone yet," Whitney snapped. "We're watching the movers in the morning."

"Are you certain that's all right with her mother?"

"Sure, why not?"

"No one wants an extra burden around when they're moving."

"Burden? Am I a burden?"

"Just stay out of everyone's way. That's all I meant."

Whitney pouted.

"Now stop sulking and come to bed. You'll be getting up early, I'm sure, to rush right over there."

*

But she didn't get up early. In fact, it was with great difficulty that she crawled out of bed at nine o'clock to get the phone.

"Where are you?" Robin barked impatiently.

"Where do you think?" she retorted, though half-asleep.

"But Whitney," Robin whined, "you're supposed to *be* here."

"I can't get up. I don't know why, but I can't."

"Well, you're up now. Get dressed and come right over."

"Meet me halfway."

Robin was silent for a minute, then she shouted to her mother. "All right." She came back on. "I'll meet you at Alden and Mountain, but you have to leave *now*."

Whitney hung up, threw on her cutoffs, and dashed out of the house. Robin wasn't at Alden, so she rode two blocks further to Birch. Still no Robin. Well, she wasn't going any further. Dropping her bike on the grass, she sat on the curb for a few minutes before her friend appeared in the distance. Robin braked her bike at Whitney's feet and jumped off. "C'mon." She extended her hand to Whitney.

Whitney didn't budge. "Where to?"

"My house."

"Is Charlotte there?"

"Sure. Everyone is."

"I don't want to."

"Whitney, you said you would."

"I changed my mind. How about riding to the park one last time?"

"I can't, Whitney. Please, don't be stubborn. Not now."

"Well, why not?" she asked, feeling herself digging in more.

"They might leave without me. I told my mother I'd be right back. You have to come. You said you would."

"How about riding around here for a while?"

"Then will you come?"

"Maybe."

They zigzagged up and down all the streets running into Mountain until they had worked their way down to Jerry's luncheonette. "We're practically at the park now," Whitney called over her shoulder. "We might as well go the rest of the way."

"We're practically at my house too. We'll go there."

Whitney braked. Robin swerved to avoid crashing into her. Their pedals locked. Whitney grabbed Robin's handlebars. Robin leapt off her seat to the street. "What did you do that for?"

"What?"

"Stop without warning me."

"I didn't mean to."

"C'mon then." Robin's voice softened. "Wait till you see the movers. One of them's real cute and very friendly. He even said we could help when they get to the lighter stuff."

"I — I have to go home."

Robin stamped her foot. "Whitney Gabriel, you promised."

"I did not, I said maybe."

"You tricked me!"

"No, I didn't."

"You never do what *I* want."

"That's not true. You won't do what I want either."

"I can't," Robin whimpered. "Don't you want to see me off?"

"Not really. I — I have other things to do."

"Whitney, I'll never speak to you again if you don't come."

"I can't, I just can't."

Robin was staring at her now. Whitney felt frightened suddenly of what life would be like without Robin. She stared at the ground, cleared her throat. "So, I guess I'll say goodbye now." She looked up into Robin's eyes — they were bright, always bright, like her mother said — and felt her own eyes clouding with tears. She looked down again. "Well, be seein' ya," she said, hoping Robin would give in and agree to go one last time to the park.

"Yeah." Robin perched back up on her bicycle seat, still looking at her funny. "See you around."

Whitney pedaled a circle around her.

"Whitney?"

Whitney stopped, turned her head eagerly. "Yeah?"

Robin's eyes were swimming now. "You sure you don't want to come watch — "

"Positive."

"Okay." Robin dried her eyes on her sleeve. "Well, so long," she said bravely.

"So long," Whitney answered, not moving as Robin wheeled slowly past her.

"Bye," Robin shouted. "I'll write!"

But Whitney didn't turn around. She pedaled up Mountain, not daring to look back, a voice inside her crying, *Don't you understand? You can't leave now. I love you.* She stopped her bike around the bend, out of sight, and looked down the deserted street. "Come back," she whispered. "Please come back." No Robin appeared around the bend. No signs of life at all.

Even then, riding up and down Mountain, her eyes filled with tears and her glasses so streaked she could barely see, she didn't know how much she was going to miss Robin, how lonely she was going to feel as Robin's letters came less and less often, how little interest she had in anything else in the world — she had never felt this way before about anybody. Nor would she have believed it if she had been told during those long summer days that before the year was out she would be spending nearly all her free time with the new boy who had moved in next door, and that by the time she finally stopped hearing from Robin she would be falling in love with someone else.